A SEASON of SECOND CHANCES

Trisha Fuentes

ARDENT ARTIST
BOOKS
PUBLISHING SINCE 2008

CW01270408

ISBN: 979-8-3306-3161-2 (Paperback)

Published by
Ardent Artist Books
www.ardentartistbooks.com

ABOUT ARDENT ARTIST BOOKS

➡ **ABOUT US**

Ardent Artist Books was established in 2008

We publish modern and historical romances once a month!

Get Your FREE List: Published & Upcoming Books
visit our website at:
https://bit.ly/3Wva400

➡ **WE HAVE BOOK TRAILERS TOO!**

Follow us on YouTube!
https://bit.ly/3W3xn7a

Like, Subscribe & Comment

➥ READ SERIALIZED FICTION!

Visit our website today to download one of our stories that unfold in bite-sized pieces!

Each installment is just 99¢!

https://bit.ly/3LsDpJL

➥ LET'S CONNECT!

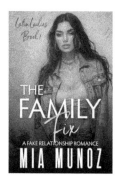

Fuel your love of fiction with exclusive content and captivating insights from Ardent Artist Books. Whether you crave the thrill of modern narratives or the timeless elegance of historical fiction, our newsletter delivers a curated selection straight to your inbox. Plus, as a welcome gift, receive a FREE downloadable eBook:

"The Family Fix"
https://bit.ly/49BR3UB

CONTENTS

CHAPTER ONE
A MOTHER'S DUTY
MAYFAIR, LONDON 1815

Morning light streamed across Grosvenor Square, warming the pale stone facades. Katherine stood at the window, remembering quiet mornings in James's study. He would read from his scientific journals, pretending not to notice how quickly she grasped the astronomical calculations. The memory brought a smile, followed by the familiar hollow ache. James had given her that rare gift—the freedom to be clever without fear of censure.

Standing at Charlotte's bedroom window, Katherine pressed her palm against the cool glass, anchoring herself in the present moment. Behind her, her daughter slumbered in a tangle of ivory silk bedding, dark curls splayed across the pillow like a halo. These quiet moments before Charlotte woke were Katherine's sanctuary—the only time she could let her carefully maintained composure slip, could be simply Katherine—rather than *Lady Ashworth*—the perfect widow and mother.

The early morning air carried the scent of spring roses from the garden below, triggering an unexpected memory: James's hands warm on her waist as they walked among the blooms, his breath against her ear as he whispered observations about the stars hiding behind the daylight. Physical intimacy had come slowly to their marriage, but those innocent touches had awakened something in her that she now missed with an intensity that frightened her.

At eight-and-thirty, Katherine was uncomfortably aware that society considered her firmly on the shelf, her role now limited to launching her daughter into the same marriage mart she had navigated two decades ago. She studied her reflection in the window glass, noting the subtle signs of strain around her eyes, the single thread of silver woven through her rich auburn hair. Her figure remained slim, her posture perfect—years of training couldn't be undone—but lately she'd caught herself wondering if anyone would ever see her as more than Charlotte's mother again.

The sound of hoofbeats drew her attention to the square below, where Lord Timothy made his now-daily ride past their house. Katherine's stomach tightened with familiar discomfort. James's older brother had been increasing his visits since her period of deep mourning ended, his concern for their welfare becoming almost suffocating. His attentions, though proper, carried an undercurrent that made her increasingly uneasy. It wasn't that Timothy wasn't an honorable man—he was. But the thought of replacing James with his brother made her physically ill.

"Charlotte, darling," Katherine kept her voice gentle, reaching for the composure she would need for the day ahead. Her fingers smoothed unconsciously over her dark blue morning dress, a habit born of years ensuring every detail was perfect. In the privacy of her thoughts, she allowed herself to remember when dressing had been for her own pleasure, not just social propriety. "It's time."

A muffled groan emerged from beneath the coverlet. "Surely not yet, Mama."

Katherine moved to the wardrobe, where the specially commissioned white silk hung like a banner of war. She ran her fingers along the delicate material, remembering her own debut season. The expectations had seemed mountainous then, but they paled in comparison to the weight she carried now. Every decision, every subtle social maneuver would affect not just Charlotte's evening, but her entire future. Sometimes, in her darkest moments, Katherine wondered if she was living too much through her daughter, pouring all her unused passion into Charlotte's debut.

"Your modiste appointment is at ten, and we still need to decide on your gown for tonight." She kept her voice steady, though her mind raced with the thousand details that must be perfect. One mistake could doom Charlotte's chances, and Katherine would rather die than fail in this maternal duty.

Charlotte bolted upright, brunette curls in disarray. "Not the white silk. It's completely wrong."

"Wrong?" Katherine's fingers stilled on the fabric, recognizing the particular pitch in Charlotte's voice that warned of a storm. In these moments, her daughter reminded her painfully of herself at eighteen—though Katherine had buried her own willful nature beneath layers of propriety long ago. "But yesterday—"

"Yesterday I hadn't heard that Isabella Fairfax is wearing white to Almack's." Charlotte's lower lip trembled in a way that was at once genuine and calculated. "Papa would have understood. He always said I should stand out."

The mention of James sent a familiar pang through Katherine's chest, sharper for being unexpected. Five years a widow, and still her husband's memory could pierce her composure like a needle through silk. She pressed her palm flat against the wardrobe, steadying herself. These days, it wasn't so much grief that undid her as the growing awareness that she had been slowly disappearing into her role as Charlotte's mother, losing pieces of herself that James had always encouraged her to nurture.

"Your father would have wanted you to make a dignified entrance into society." The words came automatically, part of the careful script she'd developed. But even as she spoke them, Katherine remembered James's quiet laughter at society's strictures, the way he'd encouraged her to read his scientific journals late at night, his pride in her quick grasp of mathematical concepts that would have scandalized the ton if they'd known.

Watching Charlotte's mounting rebellion, Katherine felt a sudden, unwelcome kinship with her daughter's desire to stand out. How long had it been since she'd allowed herself that same freedom? The astronomical calculations she still worked on in secret lay hidden in her desk drawer, alongside the letters from James's scientific colleagues who had no idea they'd been corresponding with a woman.

"The blue silk, then," Charlotte declared, throwing back her covers. "The one with the pearl trim."

Katherine drew a slow breath, tasting the familiar blend of love and frustration that seemed to flavor every interaction with her daughter lately. When had Charlotte's childhood sweetness transformed into this peculiar mixture of vulnerability and manipulation? And when had Katherine herself transformed from a woman of passionate interests into someone who measured her days in social calls and proper appearances?

Through the window, she caught another glimpse of Lord Timothy, now dismounting his horse. His gaze turned unerringly toward Charlotte's windows, and Katherine stepped back into the shadows, her skin prickling with awareness. Since James's death, Timothy's concern had grown increasingly... proprietary. He meant well, she knew, but his attention made her acutely aware of her position as a widow of still-marriageable age. The thought of accepting another man's touch, another man's claim to her body, sent tremors of distress through her entire being—yet society would expect exactly that, eventually.

"Mama! You're not listening!" Charlotte's voice cut through her reverie. "I said I won't wear the white silk. I won't!"

Katherine closed her eyes briefly, summoning patience. The real battle wasn't about the gown—it never was. Behind Charlotte's demands, Katherine recognized the same fear she herself had felt at eighteen, the terror of disappearing into society's expectations. She opened her eyes, fixing her daughter with a steady gaze that had cowed many a social upstart, though her heart ached at having to employ such tactics with her own child.

"You will go, and you will wear the white silk. However..." She paused, seeing Charlotte's mounting rebellion. "We might add your aunt's sapphire drops. They'll bring out your eyes and ensure you're not mistaken for Miss Fairfax."

The suggestion of the sapphires was a calculated risk. Katherine had worn them on her wedding night, when James's hands had trembled as he fastened them at her throat. The memory of his fingers brushing her skin sent an unexpected shiver down her spine. These days, she was touched only in the most proper ways—a gloved hand at a ball, a chaste kiss from Charlotte. The lack of physical contact was its own kind of loneliness, one she rarely allowed herself to acknowledge.

As Martha bustled in with hot water and fresh towels, the distinct voices of the Misses Bancroft carried through the window, their gossip sharp as winter wind.

> *"The Earl of Rutherford, returned after all these years..."*
> *"They say he made his fortune in China..."*
> *"Surely he'll be at Almack's tonight..."*

Katherine found herself lingering by the window, though the gossips had already moved past. *Rutherford.* The name stirred something in her memory—a scandal, perhaps? But more than that, it awakened a dangerous spark of curiosity. A gentleman who had built his own wealth, rather than simply receiving it from birth, might appreciate a sharp mind in a lady. Such a man might understand that yearning for knowledge that she concealed beneath quiet smiles and downcast eyes...

She pushed the thought away firmly, startled by its intensity. Such speculations were inappropriate for a woman in her position. Yet as she turned back to the domestic crisis at hand, she couldn't quite suppress a treacherous whisper in her mind: *When did I decide that my only passion should be ensuring Charlotte's happiness?*

Hours later, Katherine sat at her writing desk in the morning room, her fingers tracing the edge of her carefully crafted lists while Charlotte sulked on a nearby chaise. The white silk gown hung ready, the sapphire drops had been retrieved from the family vault (though touching them had sparked memories that left her oddly breathless), and all was proceeding according to plan—until Madame Delafield's message arrived, shattering her carefully constructed schedule like a porcelain cup dropped on marble.

Katherine's chest tightened as she re-read the note. *Another fitting? Impossible.* She'd spent weeks orchestrating this day with the precision of a military campaign, each hour allocated with exact purpose. *The same precision she'd once applied to astronomical calculations,* she thought wryly, in those midnight hours when James would lean over her shoulder, his warmth seeping through her dressing gown as they charted the heavens together.

"What do you mean, she needs to adjust the bodice again?" Charlotte sprang up, face flushed. "Everything was perfect yesterday!"

Katherine watched her daughter pace, seeing in her agitation echoes of her own carefully suppressed anxiety. *Perfect.* The word haunted her these days. The perfect widow, the perfect mother, the perfect example of propriety. Sometimes she longed to be perfectly imperfect, to let her mask slip just enough to reveal the woman beneath—the one who still dreamed of more than arranging marriages and managing social calendars.

"Perfection takes time, my dear." The words came out steady, practiced, though her mind was already racing through contingencies. *Would Lady Jersey notice if they arrived a quarter-hour later than the precise moment of fashionable arrival? Would the delay affect Charlotte's chances with potential suitors? Would anyone see past Charlotte to notice Katherine's own careful perfection, the way James once had?*

As they prepared to leave, Mrs. Davis appeared in the doorway, her usually unflappable demeanor showing signs of strain. "Begging your pardon, my lady, but the Dowager Countess of Rutherford has sent her card. She's in the drawing room."

Katherine's heart stuttered. *The Dowager Countess?* Of all days for one of the Almack's patronesses to make an unexpected call —and this particular patroness, when gossip about her son was already circulating through London like wildfire.

She pressed her fingers to her temple, feeling the beginning of a headache. The social calculations whirled through her mind, but beneath them ran a current of unwelcome awareness. *Would the Dowager see past her widow's perfect propriety?*

"Tell her we're just leaving for an urgent appointment," she began, but Charlotte interrupted, her tears mysteriously vanished.

"The Dowager Countess? Isn't she one of the Almack's patronesses?"

Katherine's gaze fell on her daughter, suddenly seeing with painful clarity how much of herself she'd poured into Charlotte's debut. Not just her time and energy, but her own suppressed desires for recognition, for passion, for a life beyond society's narrow boundaries. *Was she using Charlotte's Season to relive her own youth, or to avoid facing her future?*

As they made their way to the drawing room, Katherine squared her shoulders, feeling the familiar weight of her responsibilities settle around her like a heavy cloak. She'd spent the five years since James's death ensuring their social position remained impeccable, building a fortress of respectability around herself and Charlotte. But standing before the drawing-room door, she suddenly wondered if she'd built a prison instead.

"Mama?" Charlotte's voice was suddenly small, more like the little girl she'd been than the debutante she was becoming. "What if she doesn't approve of me?"

Katherine stopped, turning to study her daughter. Behind Charlotte's carefully arranged expression, she saw real fear flickering. For a moment, all her frustrations melted away. This was why she did it all—the endless social maneuvering, the constant vigilance, the suppression of her own feelings. Not for society's approval, but for this beautiful, difficult, wonderful girl who still needed her mother's protection.

Yet even as she reached to adjust one of Charlotte's curls, Katherine felt the stirring of something new. Perhaps it was the gossip about the Earl, or the memory of James's encouragement of her hidden talents, or simply the accumulation of five years of carefully contained loneliness. But suddenly she knew that while she would always be Charlotte's mother, perhaps it was time to remember how to be Katherine as well.

"My darling," she said softly, "she would have to be blind, deaf, and thoroughly lacking in sense not to see your worth." She allowed herself a small smile, feeling the unfamiliar muscles stretch. "Now, shall we show her exactly why the Ashworth women are considered among the ton's finest?"

CHAPTER TWO
ALMACK'S

Katherine's fingers tightened on Charlotte's arm as their carriage joined the queue outside Almack's. The line of elegant carriages stretched into the misty evening like a string of black pearls, each one carrying its own cargo of hopes and schemes. Through the window, the famous façade loomed, its windows glowing with promise—or warning.

"Remember, darling," Katherine murmured, though her racing thoughts made it difficult to focus on the familiar devotion. "Lady Jersey will be watching from the moment we—"

"I know, Mama." Charlotte's voice carried an edge that made Katherine glance sharply at her daughter. In the shadowed interior of the carriage, Charlotte's face held the same mutinous expression she'd worn during their argument over the white silk gown. "You've told me a thousand times."

And I'll tell you a thousand more if it keeps you safe, Katherine thought, but held her tongue. Instead, she found herself remembering her own debut, how James had later told her he'd first noticed her here, standing nervously in line for Lady Jersey's approval. His gentle humor had eased her terror then. Now, after five years without his steadying presence, she felt that same terror rising again—not for herself this time, but for Charlotte.

The carriage lurched to a stop. Through the window, Katherine caught a glimpse of Isabella Fairfax ascending the steps in white silk that made her look washed out. A small, unworthy spark of satisfaction flickered in Katherine's chest—Charlotte's white silk was a different matter entirely, especially with the sapphire drops casting subtle blue lights against her throat.

"Lady Katherine?" The footman's voice startled her from the memory. "We've arrived."

Gathering her composure like a cloak, Katherine descended from the carriage, every movement calculated to convey graceful assurance. As Charlotte followed, Katherine allowed herself one brief moment of pride. Whatever her daughter's temperamental moments in private, she moved now with perfect poise, head held at exactly the right angle to suggest confidence without arrogance.

Then Charlotte gasped.

Katherine followed her daughter's gaze to where a rival debutante was entering Almack's, wearing a gown that, while not identical to Charlotte's, shared an unmistakable similarity in its pearl trim and delicate embroidery.

"Mama!" Charlotte's whisper held the same sharp edge that had preceded countless childhood tantrums. "That horrid Andrews girl is wearing—"

"Is wearing a gown that only serves to highlight how superior yours is," Katherine cut in smoothly, though her heart had begun to race. This was exactly the sort of crisis that could shatter a debutante's composure—and with it, her chances. "Notice how the pearls on her trim are irregular? And that embroidery was clearly done by a country seamstress."

The subtle curl of Charlotte's lip told Katherine her quick save had worked, but the victory felt hollow. *When had she become so adept at these little cruelties?* James would have been disappointed in her. Yet as she guided Charlotte toward the entrance, Katherine couldn't quite suppress the thought that James had never truly understood the brutal mathematics of the marriage mart, where one wrong step could destroy a girl's chances forever.

They were halfway up the steps when Katherine felt it—that peculiar sensation of being watched that she'd developed over twenty years in society. She turned her head slightly, superficially to adjust Charlotte's shawl, and caught her first clear glimpse of him.

The Earl of Rutherford stood near the entrance, his broad shoulders and commanding presence making the younger lords around him look like boys playing at being men. His dark hair was shot with distinguished silver at the temples, his face tanned in a way that spoke of real exposure to sun and wind rather than mere fashion. But it was his eyes that caught and held Katherine's attention—sharp, grey, and utterly focused on her.

Katherine's breath caught as fragments of memory surfaced. Lord Rutherford—Marcus, as she'd heard him called then—at Lady Worthington's musical evening twelve years ago. James had been particularly interested in his tales of the China trade, while Katherine had found herself captivated by the way his hands moved as he described the foreign ports he planned to visit.

"Your husband has excellent taste in business ventures," he'd told her that evening, his grey eyes warm with approval. "Though I confess, I'm surprised more gentlemen don't take an interest in the opportunities in the East."

The next morning, he'd sailed for China. James had occasionally mentioned letters from him over the years, discussing investments and trade routes, but Katherine had filed away the memory of those hands, that voice, as nothing more than a passing fancy.

Now, standing on the steps of Almack's with her daughter's future hanging in the balance, Katherine found herself unable to look away from him. The years abroad had transformed him from a merely handsome man into something altogether more dangerous. The sharp angles of his face had weathered into fascinating planes and shadows, and his bearing spoke of a man who had faced real challenges rather than merely inherited his position.

"Mama?" Charlotte tugged at her arm. "Why are you dawdling?"

Katherine forced her attention back to her daughter, though she remained acutely aware of Lord Rutherford's presence. "I'm merely ensuring we make an appropriate entrance, darling. One must pause occasionally to allow others to notice one's arrival."

"Well, I believe that gentleman has noticed quite enough," Charlotte said with a hint of spite that made Katherine's cheeks warm. "Though surely he's too old to be of any interest to anyone."

The words stung more than they should have. Katherine straightened her spine, letting her fingers rest lightly on the banister as they continued their ascent. "Lord Rutherford is one of the ton's most influential peers, Charlotte. You would do well to remember that wealth and connections often matter more than youth."

"Lord Rutherford?" Charlotte's tone shifted from dismissive to calculating so quickly it made Katherine's head spin. "The one who's been away in China? Lady Jersey mentioned him just last week. She said he's seeking a wife."

Something cold and heavy settled in Katherine's stomach. Of course, he would be seeking a wife. A man of his position needed an heir, and after so many years abroad, he would be expected to settle down with someone young enough to provide one. Someone exactly Charlotte's age.

The thought shouldn't have bothered her. She'd spent the past five years focused solely on preparing Charlotte for precisely this sort of opportunity. Yet as they passed Lord Rutherford on their way inside, and Katherine caught the subtle scent of sandalwood and leather that clung to him, she found herself fighting an entirely inappropriate surge of disappointment.

"Lady Ashworth." His voice was deeper than she remembered, with a richness that sent an unexpected shiver down her spine. "I had heard you would be here tonight."

Katherine turned, careful to keep her expression composed. "Lord Rutherford. Welcome back to England." She gestured to Charlotte, who had already arranged her features into their most becoming smile. "May I present my daughter, Miss Ashworth?"

"Enchanted." He bowed over Charlotte's hand, but his eyes flickered back to Katherine. "Your mother and I are old acquaintances, Miss Ashworth. Though I fear I left for China before you were old enough to remember me."

"How fascinating," Charlotte breathed, and Katherine recognized the practiced tone that had already wrapped half the ton's eligible young men around her finger. "You must tell me all about your adventures, my lord. I find foreign lands absolutely thrilling."

But Lord Rutherford's attention had already shifted back to Katherine. "I was sorry to hear about James," he said quietly. "He was a good man."

The genuine warmth in his voice caught her off guard. "Yes," she managed. "He was."

"Lady Katherine." Lady Jersey's cool voice snapped Katherine back to her duties. "How good of you to bring your daughter tonight."

Katherine executed a perfect curtsey, gratified to see Charlotte mirror her movements exactly. As she straightened, she forced herself to focus on the patroness's face rather than letting her gaze drift to where she could still feel Rutherford watching. She had a role to play, after all. A duty to fulfill.

But for the first time in five years, duty felt like a cage rather than a comfort.

Lady Jersey's grip on Charlotte's arm was feather-light but inexorable as she guided them through the crowd. Katherine followed a precise two steps behind, close enough to intervene if needed but far enough to give Charlotte room to shine. From this vantage point, she could observe how the candlelight caught the sapphires at her daughter's throat, making them wink like stars.

"Lord Ridlington," Lady Jersey called out to a tall young man standing near one of the marble columns. "I simply must introduce you to Miss Ashworth."

The young man turned, revealing a handsome face with kind hazel eyes. His grandmother, the Dowager Lady Ridlington, hovered nearby with an expression that suggested she'd orchestrated this introduction through careful manipulation of Lady Jersey's legendary matchmaking tendencies.

"Miss Ashworth," Lord Ridlington bowed, his movements graceful despite what appeared to be barely concealed exhaustion. "I've heard much about your debut."

Charlotte's curtsey was perfect, but Katherine noticed the slight tightening around her daughter's mouth that suggested she found him lacking. "How kind of you to say so, my lord. Though I cannot imagine what you might have heard, as this is my first proper appearance."

"My grandmother speaks highly of your accomplishments," he offered, though his smile seemed directed more at being polite than any genuine interest.

Before Charlotte could respond, Lady Jersey was already steering her toward their next introduction. "Lord and Lady Winter, do allow me to present Miss Ashworth."

The Winter family stood in their usual formation – Lord Winter looking severe, Lady Winter attempting to appear less severe, and their son Charles wearing an expression of such studied boredom that Katherine wondered if he practiced it in the mirror.

"Charmed," Charles drawled, managing to make the word sound anything but.

Charlotte's responding smile held a hint of frost. "Indeed."

Lady Jersey, perhaps sensing the temperature dropping around them, quickly moved them along to their final introduction. "Ah, Mr. and Mrs. Carmichael! And young Mr. Carmichael, of course. This is Miss Ashworth."

Katherine watched as Albert Carmichael stepped forward, his light brown hair artfully tousled and his blue eyes sparkling with barely contained mischief. His bow was exactly correct, yet somehow managed to suggest he found the whole ritual amusing.

"Miss Ashworth," his voice carried a warmth his predecessors had lacked. "I must say, the rumors of your beauty did not do you justice."

For the first time that evening, Charlotte's smile reached her eyes. "How forward of you, Mr. Carmichael. I believe my mother would say such direct compliments are hardly proper."

"Then it's fortunate that my family's fortune comes from trade rather than titles. We're allowed to be a bit more direct, aren't we?" He winked, and Katherine felt her stomach clench with worry.

Mr. Carmichael senior stepped forward, his expression suggesting he'd heard similar exchanges from his son before. "Perhaps you might honor us with a dance later, Miss Ashworth? If your card isn't already full?"

"I believe I might have a space or two remaining," Charlotte replied, though Katherine knew for a fact her daughter's dance card was entirely empty.

As they moved away, Katherine caught Charlotte studying Albert Carmichael's retreating figure with far more interest than she'd shown the other young men. The set of her daughter's shoulders, the slight lift of her chin—Katherine recognized the signs. Charlotte had decided Mr. Carmichael would make an entertaining pursuit, regardless of his suitability.

"Well," Lady Jersey pronounced, "that should give you quite a nice start for your first evening. Though I must say, Lord Ridlington would be an excellent match. His estate borders your family's lands in Hampshire, does it not?"

"It does," Katherine confirmed, though she'd noticed how Lord Ridlington's attention had seemed divided, his eyes constantly darting to the entrance as though expecting someone. "Though perhaps it might be best to let Charlotte become better acquainted with all the young men before forming any particular attachments."

Lady Jersey's eyebrow arched. "One must strike while the iron is hot, Lady Ashworth. Surely you remember that from your own Season?"

Before Katherine could respond, the musicians began tuning their instruments for the first dance. Charlotte's fingers tightened on her fan, her eyes fixed on where Albert Carmichael stood chatting with a group of young men.

"Mama," Charlotte whispered, "do make sure Mr. Carmichael knows I expect him to claim that dance he mentioned."

Katherine suppressed a sigh. Of all the eligible young men they'd just met, of course Charlotte would fix her interest on the one most likely to cause gossip. "Perhaps we should wait to see who approaches you, darling. Too much eagerness can be unseemly."

But Charlotte's attention had already wandered, her eyes following Albert Carmichael's movements with the intensity of a cat watching a particularly interesting bird. Katherine recognized that look all too well—it was the same one Charlotte had worn before every childhood escapade that had ended in disaster.

Katherine positioned herself at the perfect vantage point—close enough to monitor Charlotte without appearing to hover, far enough from the dance floor to discourage potential suitors of her own. From here, she could orchestrate her daughter's evening while maintaining the illusion that Charlotte navigated the social waters independently.

Yet her usually sharp focus kept slipping, drawn inexorably to the tall figure now conversing with Lady Jersey. The Earl of Rutherford moved with the easy grace of a man comfortable in his own skin, so different from the posturing youngsters who populated Almack's. Katherine found herself studying the way his evening clothes sat on his broad shoulders, wondering what it might feel like to—

"Lady Ashworth." The silken voice sliced through her inappropriate musings. "How delightful to see you out of mourning at last."

Katherine turned to find Lady Constance Whitmore beside her, resplendent in a gown of deep crimson that bordered on scandalous. The widow's perfectly arranged blonde curls and porcelain complexion belied the predatory gleam in her eyes.

"Lady Constance," Katherine inclined her head precisely the correct degree for greeting a social equal whom one privately disdained. "How kind of you to notice."

"One notices all sorts of things," Lady Constance's gaze drifted deliberately toward Rutherford. "The return of eligible gentlemen to society, for instance. Though perhaps such matters interest you less these days, focused as you are on your maternal duties."

The subtle barb struck its target—Katherine's lingering awareness of her own desirability—but years of social warfare had taught her to smile through deeper wounds. "Indeed, Charlotte's debut consumes much of my attention." She paused, then added with perfectly calculated concern, "Though I'm sure you need no reminder of the challenges of a first Season. How many years has it been since your own debut? Time does fly so."

A flash of genuine anger crossed Lady Constance's face before her mask slipped back into place. "Speaking of time, I see the Dowager Countess beckoning. Do excuse me."

As her rival glided away, Katherine released a careful breath. The exchange had been a minor victory, but it left a sour taste in her mouth. *When had she become so adept at these subtle cruelties?* James would have—but no, she couldn't keep measuring herself against James's memory, especially not tonight when her body hummed with an awareness she hadn't felt in years.

"Mama!" Charlotte materialized at her elbow, cheeks flushed with excitement or frustration—with Charlotte, the two often looked identical. "Lord Ridlington hasn't claimed his set yet, and he promised..."

Katherine forced her attention back to the intricate dance of managing Charlotte's partners, though she remained acutely aware of Rutherford's presence across the room. She felt him watching her as she smoothly intervened in a near-disaster over the supper dance, as she deftly steered Charlotte away from an inappropriate conversation with Lord Winter's rakish son, as she maintained her perfect widow's smile through it all.

The evening air grew heavy with the press of bodies and expectations. Katherine found herself longing for the cool night breeze and the comfort of her astronomical calculations. Here, surrounded by the ton's finest, she felt more alone than she did in her study with only the stars for company.

"He's quite magnificent, isn't he?" The Dowager Countess of Rutherford appeared at Katherine's side, her shrewd eyes missing nothing. "My son has grown into his position, though London society may find him... unconventional."

Katherine's heart skipped at the word 'son,' though she kept her expression neutral. "I'm sure the ton will adapt to his presence, your Grace."

"The question, my dear," the Dowager said with a hint of amusement, "is whether he will adapt to them. Marcus has little patience for our more... restrictive conventions."

Marcus. The casual use of his given name sent an unexpected shiver down Katherine's spine. She hadn't allowed herself to think of him so intimately, even in her own mind. Yet now the name echoed there, dangerous as forbidden astronomy texts.

"If you'll excuse me," Katherine murmured, suddenly desperate for air, for space, for a moment to collect herself. "I believe I see Charlotte in need of my attention."

She moved away with perfect grace, but her composure felt as fragile as spun glass. The crush of the ballroom pressed in around her, and she found herself seeking refuge in a lesser-used hallway, away from the heat and music and watching eyes.

CHAPTER THREE
QUIET REFLECTION

I n the relative quiet, Katherine pressed a hand to her throat, where her pulse raced beneath her fingers. *What was happening to her carefully ordered world?* One man's presence shouldn't be able to shake five years of carefully maintained widowhood, shouldn't make her skin feel too tight, shouldn't make her wonder about unconventional men and their views on unconventional women who studied the stars...

She was so lost in her thoughts that she didn't hear the approaching footsteps until it was too late.

The collision was both literal and symbolic—her careful world crashing into something altogether more dangerous. Strong hands steadied her before she could stumble, and Katherine found herself looking up into the grey eyes that had haunted her throughout the evening.

"My apologies, my lady," his voice was deep, touched with an accent that hinted at years abroad. "Though perhaps fate has conspired to arrange this meeting."

Katherine was acutely aware of his hands on her arms, the heat of them burning through her silk sleeves. *How long had it been since a man had touched her with such casual strength?* The realization that she'd been unconsciously counting the years made her step back, though her body protested the loss of contact.

"Fate seems to have poor timing, my lord," she managed, proud that her voice remained steady despite her thundering heart. "I was merely seeking a moment's air."

"As was I." Rutherford—*Marcus,* her treacherous mind whispered—made no move to leave. Instead, he studied her with an intensity that made her feel seen in a way she hadn't experienced since James. "The ton's entertainments seem rather... stifling after years at sea."

The word 'stifling' resonated through her like a struck bell. *How many times had she thought the same, while maintaining her perfect widow's smile?* "I would imagine the ocean offers more freedom than Almack's," she said, then nearly bit her tongue. *What was she doing, encouraging this conversation?*

"Freedom, danger, discovery," his lips curved slightly. "Though I suspect you know something about discovery yourself, Lady Ashworth. I couldn't help but notice your reaction when my mother mentioned conventional behavior."

Heat bloomed in her cheeks. "You presume much, my lord, on such brief acquaintance."

"Do I?" He took a step closer, not quite improper but certainly not entirely proper either. "Then why are you hiding in this hallway instead of performing your maternal duties?"

The question struck uncomfortably close to her earlier thoughts. "I am not hiding," she protested, though the words felt hollow. "I am simply..."

"Seeking freedom? Discovery? A moment without society's weight on your shoulders?" Each suggestion brought him slightly closer, until she could detect the faint scent of sandalwood and something uniquely male that made her head spin. "Tell me, my lady, do you ever tire of being exactly what everyone expects?"

"I..." Katherine's carefully constructed responses deserted her. In their place rose dangerous truths: *Yes, I tire of it. Yes, I long for freedom. Yes, I want to be seen as more than a widow, more than a mother, more than a perfect pattern card of propriety.*

The sound of approaching voices saved her from replying. She stepped back quickly, smoothing her skirts with trembling hands. "We shouldn't..."

"Be discovered in conversation? How shocking," his voice held a trace of mockery, but his eyes were intense, almost angry. "That we must pretend this encounter never happened, that two adults cannot share a moment of honest discourse—is this not exactly the stifling convention I spoke of?"

"You've been away too long," Katherine said softly. "You've forgotten how reputations are built and destroyed here. My daughter's future—"

"Ah yes, your daughter." Something flickered in his expression. "The lovely Miss Ashworth, around whom your world revolves. Tell me, Lady Ashworth, do you ever allow yourself to revolve around something else? The stars, perhaps?"

Katherine's breath caught. *How could he know about her astronomical interests? Had his mother somehow...?*

The voices grew closer. Any moment now, they would be discovered. Scandal would ensue. Charlotte's chances would be ruined. Katherine's carefully ordered world would shatter.

"Good evening, my lord," she said firmly, gathering her composure like armor. "I must return to my duties."

She turned to leave, but his voice followed her, low and intimate: "Running away, Katherine?"

The use of her given name stopped her mid-step. No one had spoken it in that tone, with that hint of masculine appreciation, since James. She looked back despite herself.

"Not running," she corrected quietly. "Choosing. As I must."

But even as she walked away, head high and steps measured, she knew something fundamental had shifted. The Katherine who entered that hallway was not quite the same as the one leaving it. And judging by the weight of his gaze on her back, the Earl of Rutherford knew it too.

Marcus watched Katherine's retreating form, admiring how she managed to inject both grace and purpose into her escape. The silk of her deep blue gown whispered against the floor, and he clenched his fist to keep from reaching after her.

Blast it all. He hadn't expected this visceral reaction to James Ashworth's widow. The memory of their first meeting rose unbidden—a garden party at his mother's estate seven years ago, just before he'd sailed for China. Katherine had worn lavender that day, her auburn hair catching the sunlight as she bent to examine one of his mother's prized roses. Even then, something about her had caught his attention.

James had been alive then, hovering at her elbow like a proud gardener showing off his most precious bloom. But Marcus had noticed the way Katherine's eyes had strayed to the astronomy texts he'd left on the garden table, the quick flash of intelligence before she'd smoothed her features back into socially acceptable mild interest.

"Remarkable woman," James had said later over brandy. "Too clever by half, but she hides it well."

Marcus released a slow breath, adjusting his cravat which had grown uncomfortably tight. Katherine was even more alluring now than she'd been then. The years had added character to her beauty, like fine wine reaching its perfect moment. The reserved widow's facade couldn't quite hide the passionate nature beneath—he'd seen it in the way her pulse had jumped at her throat when he'd steadied her, in the slight parting of her lips when he'd spoken her Christian name.

"There you are, Rutherford." His mother's voice cut through his musings. She approached with her usual imperial bearing, fan tapping against her palm. "Lady Jersey has been asking after you. Something about her niece requiring a dance partner."

Marcus suppressed a groan. "Another debutante? Mother, I thought we agreed—"

"We agreed you needed to marry. I don't recall specifying an age." Her shrewd eyes narrowed. "Though I noticed you seemed rather captivated by Lady Ashworth earlier."

"Katherine is..." He caught himself using her given name and cleared his throat. "Lady Ashworth is an old acquaintance."

"Hmm," His mother's fan stilled. "A respectable widow with an excellent understanding of society. Well-connected. Still quite handsome."

"Mother."

"And more importantly, intelligent enough to manage both you and that shipping empire of yours." She tapped his arm with her fan. "Don't look so shocked, dear. I'm not nearly as conventional as I pretend to be."

Marcus studied his mother's face, seeing the calculation there. "You orchestrated this evening, didn't you? The morning call to the Ashworths, the careful mentions of my return..."

"I merely created an opportunity. What you do with it is entirely your affair." She gestured toward the ballroom. "Though if you're interested in my opinion, I'd say Lady Ashworth could use someone to remind her she's more than just Miss Charlotte's mother."

The mention of Charlotte sobered him. Katherine's daughter represented a significant complication—a spoiled girl who clearly viewed her mother as personal property.

"The ton expects me to pursue a young bride," he said, voicing the practical concern.

His mother's laugh was sharp. "The ton expects all sorts of things, dear. That doesn't mean we must bow to their expectations. Now, shall we return to the ballroom? Lady Jersey really is looking for you, and it wouldn't do to seem too obvious in your... interests."

Marcus offered his arm, his thoughts still lingering on the way Katherine had trembled ever so slightly under his touch. Seven years ago, she'd been a beautiful woman trapped in a marriage of convenience. Now she was free, but had bound herself just as thoroughly with maternal duty and social expectations.

"You're plotting," his mother observed as they walked. "I know that expression."

"Not plotting." Marcus straightened his shoulders, already formulating approaches and strategies. "Planning."

K atherine's return to the ballroom felt like stepping onto unstable ground. The familiar scene—Charlotte surrounded by admirers, Lady Jersey surveying her domain, young ladies fluttering fans in practiced allure— seemed suddenly artificial, like actors performing on a stage. Her skin still tingled where Rutherford had touched her, and his use of her given name echoed in her mind like a forbidden prayer.

Focus, she commanded herself. *Charlotte needs you.* But even as she moved to intercept an approaching rake whose reputation made him unsuitable for her daughter's dance card, Katherine found her thoughts straying to grey eyes and challenging words. *Do you ever tire of being exactly what everyone expects?*

"Mama!" Charlotte's voice, pitched higher than usual, cut through her dangerous musings. "Lord Ridlington hasn't appeared for his set, and it's nearly time!"

Katherine assessed the situation quickly, noting her daughter's rising panic. The supper dance was crucial—being left without a partner would be social suicide. Yet even as she prepared to smooth over this crisis, she caught Rutherford watching her from across the room. The weight of his gaze made her increasingly aware of her body, of the way her blue silk gown shaped her figure, of how long it had been since she'd felt truly desired...

"Lady Ashworth." Lord Timothy materialized at her elbow, his familiar presence both comfort and constraint. "Perhaps I might claim the honor of dancing with my niece?"

The solution was perfect—too perfect. Katherine felt a flash of irritation at Timothy's hovering protection, even as social necessity made her grateful for it. "How kind of you to offer, my lord. Charlotte would be delighted."

But Charlotte's expression suggested anything but delight. "But Mama, Lord Ridlington promised—"

"And has proven himself unreliable," Katherine cut in smoothly, though her voice held an edge she couldn't quite suppress. *Was she truly angry at Lord Ridlington's defection, or at her own unsettling response to a few moments with Rutherford?* "Your uncle's offer is most generous."

As Timothy led a sulking Charlotte onto the dance floor, Katherine became aware of Lady Constance advancing with obvious intent. The widow's crimson gown seemed even more provocative than before, and her destination was clear—Rutherford stood conversing with a group of gentlemen near the card room.

Something hot and unfamiliar flared in Katherine's chest. Jealousy? Impossible. She had no claim on the Earl, no right to feel possessive after one improper conversation in a hallway. Yet watching Lady Constance sway toward him with practiced seduction, Katherine felt an almost overwhelming urge to intervene.

"He won't be interested." The Dowager Countess's voice startled her. The older woman had appeared silently at Katherine's side, her shrewd eyes missing nothing. "My son has little patience for obvious manipulation."

"I'm sure I don't know what you mean, your Grace." The words came automatically, though Katherine's heart raced at this second reference to Rutherford's preferences.

"Don't you?" The Dowager's fan moved in elegant punctuation. "Just as you don't know why he's been watching you all evening? Or why he followed you into that hallway?"

Heat bloomed in Katherine's cheeks. "You saw—"

"I see everything, my dear. It's the privilege of age and rank." The Dowager's eyes sparkled with something that might have been mischief. "Just as I see your daughter creating what promises to be a magnificent scene by the supper table."

Katherine's head whipped around. Charlotte stood with a group of debutantes, her voice carrying just a touch too loudly as she declared her opinion of Lord Ridlington's character. Nearby, Lady Jersey's expression grew thunderous.

"If you'll excuse me, your Grace." Katherine moved swiftly toward the impending disaster, her mind already crafting ways to minimize the damage. Yet even as she prepared to salvage her daughter's social prospects, she felt Rutherford's gaze following her progress across the room. More disturbing still, she felt her own body responding to that attention, awakening to possibilities she'd thought long buried.

She reached Charlotte just as her daughter's voice rose dangerously higher. "Darling," she murmured, laying a gentle hand on Charlotte's arm. "Perhaps we might step out for a moment? The heat is quite overwhelming."

But before she could guide Charlotte to safety, Lady Constance's voice cut through the general murmur: "My lord Rutherford, surely you'll partner me for supper? We have so much to discuss about your fascinating experiences abroad..."

Katherine didn't mean to look. She absolutely forbade herself to turn. Yet somehow her head moved of its own accord, just in time to see Rutherford's response.

Marcus watched Katherine guide her daughter toward their waiting carriage, her practiced smile never wavering. The faint glow of street lamps caught the auburn highlights in her hair, and he found himself taking a step forward before he caught himself.

"Magnificent creature, isn't she?" Lady Jersey materialized at his elbow. "Though perhaps not what you're seeking, Rutherford? The ton expects you to choose someone more... suitable to your position."

He turned to the Almack's patroness with a carefully bland expression. "And what position would that be, madam?"

"An earl newly returned to society requires a young bride to establish his nursery, does he not?" She tapped her fan against her palm. "Lady Constance has made her interest clear."

"Has she indeed?" Marcus kept his tone mild, though his jaw tightened. Through the windows, he could see Katherine's careful posture as she settled Charlotte into the carriage. Lord Timothy Ashworth hovered nearby, his protective stance speaking volumes.

"Come now, you can't mean to waste your time pursuing a widow devoted to launching her daughter?" Lady Jersey's voice held equal measures of amusement and warning. "Katherine Ashworth hasn't spared a thought for romance since her husband's death. All of society knows she lives solely for that girl."

Marcus caught a final glimpse of Katherine's profile as the carriage pulled away. "Perhaps that's precisely what makes her interesting, Lady Jersey. If you'll excuse me?"

He made his way through the thinning crowd, nodding to acquaintances while avoiding Lady Constance's determined approach. His mind kept returning to that moment in the hallway—Katherine's startled gasp when they collided, the way her green eyes had widened in recognition of something that mirrored his own surprise. She'd felt it too, that instant of connection that defied social constraints and proper behavior.

"Brother!" Thomas Pembroke's voice cut through his reverie. "I've been looking everywhere for you. The situation in Canton requires immediate attention."

Marcus suppressed a sigh. "Surely it can wait until morning?"

"I'm afraid not." Thomas lowered his voice. "The latest dispatch arrived an hour ago. Our agent hints at irregularities in the accounts."

"Very well." Marcus cast a final glance toward the door where Katherine had disappeared. Business before pleasure—it had been his motto for twenty years. Yet somehow, tonight, the familiar phrase rang hollow.

CHAPTER FOUR
MORNING CALLS

Katherine's fingers trembled slightly as she arranged the morning room's calling cards with mathematical precision. Each rectangle of cream-colored paper represented a carefully timed social obligation for Charlotte's debut week—and a potential encounter with the Earl of Rutherford.

"Mama, surely we needn't call on old Lady Millicent first?" Charlotte's voice carried a note of petulance that made Katherine's shoulders tense. "The Bancroft sisters mentioned that Lord Pembroke's mother is receiving today, and you know he danced with me twice at Almack's."

Katherine arranged the final calling card with deliberate care, using the moment to school her features before turning to face her daughter. The mere mention of Lord Pembroke sent an uncomfortable flutter through her stomach. Of all the eligible gentlemen at Almack's, Charlotte had to set her cap at the Earl of Rutherford's cousin.

"Lady Millicent's good opinion can make or break a young lady's first Season," Katherine said, smoothing her dove-grey silk skirts. "Her morning calls are legendary for determining which debutantes will succeed."

Charlotte's lower lip protruded in a manner that reminded Katherine forcefully of her daughter at age five. "But Lord Pembroke specifically mentioned hoping to see me again soon."

"Thomas Pembroke's attention, while flattering, does not supersede the basic rules of society." Katherine picked up her silver card case, its familiar weight anchoring her against the tide of anxiety rising in her chest. The thought of Charlotte becoming entangled with the Pembroke family while she harbored these unsettling feelings for the Earl made her distinctly uneasy.

"You're being impossible," Charlotte dropped onto the settee with rather more force than necessary. "I thought you wanted me to make an advantageous match."

"I want you to make a suitable match," Katherine corrected. The distinction felt important, though she couldn't quite articulate why. Her memories of the Earl's intense grey eyes during their hallway encounter at Almack's threatened to distract her. "Lord Pembroke has something of a reputation for—"

"For what?" Charlotte sat up straighter, curiosity brightening her features. "Do tell me he has a scandalous past. That would make him ever so much more interesting."

Katherine pressed her fingers to her temple. "For being rather more focused on business ventures than establishing a proper household." The rumors of financial impropriety that had followed Lord Pembroke from the Far East remained unspoken.

"But isn't that what made the Earl so wealthy? And nobody seems to hold his years in trade against him."

"The Earl of Rutherford and his cousin are very different men." Katherine turned to adjust her bonnet in the mirror, using the moment to compose herself. She couldn't very well explain that the Earl's commanding presence and quiet intelligence bore little resemblance to his cousin's rather mercenary nature.

"They're both rich," Charlotte said with the blithe confidence of youth. "And Lord Pembroke is much closer to my age than the Earl."

Katherine's hands stilled on her bonnet ribbons. "The Earl's age has nothing to do with this discussion."

"I only meant that he's likely looking for someone more..." Charlotte paused delicately. "Someone more established in society. Like yourself, Mama."

The suggestion sent a jolt through Katherine's chest. She turned to face her daughter, careful to keep her expression neutral. "The Earl of Rutherford's matrimonial prospects are hardly our concern. Now, shall we proceed to Lady Millicent's, or shall we waste the entire morning discussing the Pembroke family?"

Charlotte rose with a dramatic sigh. "Very well. Though I still think Lord Pembroke's mother would be a more advantageous first call."

"Lady Millicent first," Katherine said firmly, leading the way to the front door where Jenkins waited with their pelisses. She refused to acknowledge the way her pulse quickened at the thought that the Earl might be calling on his aunt today as well. Her priority had to be Charlotte's successful launch into society, not her own unexpected attraction to a man who had already caused her daughter to make pointed comments about age and suitability.

As they settled into their carriage, Katherine found herself wondering if perhaps she should encourage Charlotte's interest in Lord Pembroke after all. It might be the simplest way to ensure she kept her distance from the Earl, whose mere presence seemed to wake something in her she'd thought long dormant.

T he morning sunlight streaming through the tall windows caught the gilt edges of the mirror above the fireplace, momentarily dazzling Katherine's eyes. Or perhaps it was the memory of Marcus Rutherford's intense gaze across the ballroom that made her vision swim.

Dear Lord, I'm behaving like a green girl rather than a woman grown with a daughter to launch. Katherine pressed her fingertips to her temple, willing away the memory of how Marcus's deep voice had resonated through her when he'd discussed the stars. The way his grey eyes had held hers, seeing past the careful maternal mask to the woman beneath...

Stop this foolishness at once. She straightened her spine, focusing on the neat array of calling cards before her. Each one represented a carefully cultivated connection, a potential alliance for Charlotte's future. That was what mattered—not the way her skin had tingled when Marcus's sleeve had brushed hers in that quiet hallway, or how his quiet laugh had awakened something she'd thought long dormant.

James would want me to focus on Charlotte. The thought of her late husband brought both guilt and an unexpected flash of defiance. James had always encouraged her intellectual pursuits, even when society raised its collective eyebrows at a viscountess who read scientific papers. Would he truly want her to deny this connection, this chance at—

No. I won't even think that word. Love was for the young, for debutantes with their whole lives ahead of them. Not for widowed mothers who knew better than to risk their daughters' futures on selfish impulses.

Besides, what could a worldly man like Marcus Rutherford want with a woman whose life revolved around managing her daughter's social calendar? Even if his eyes had lit up when she'd mentioned her theories about stellar parallax, even if he'd leaned in close enough that she could catch the faint scent of sandalwood...

"Lady Millicent's good opinion can make or break a young lady's reputation in society," Katherine replied, keeping her voice steady. "And as she was kind enough to sponsor your vouchers for Almack's..."

A soft knock interrupted them as Mrs. Davis appeared with a fresh pot of tea. "Begging your pardon, my lady, but the Dowager Countess of Rutherford's carriage has just turned into the square."

Katherine's heart performed an entirely improper flutter. *Surely Marcus wouldn't accompany his mother on morning calls?* Yet her eyes strayed to the mirror, checking that every auburn curl was perfectly in place.

The Dowager swept into the morning room moments later, her elegant grey silk rustling with authority. "My dear Lady Ashworth, Miss Charlotte." Her sharp eyes missed nothing as she settled into the chosen chair. "I trust you've recovered from the excitement of Almack's?"

"Oh, yes!" Charlotte brightened immediately. "Lord Pembroke said my dancing was the most accomplished he'd seen this Season, and—"

"Indeed." The Dowager's tone held a note that made Charlotte falter. "Though I observed you seemed rather short of breath during the supper dance. One must pace oneself during these early weeks, my dear."

Katherine watched her daughter's cheeks flush pink. The girl wasn't used to anything less than effusive praise, and the Dowager's gentle criticism clearly stung.

"I'm sure Charlotte will learn to manage her energies better as the Season progresses," Katherine offered diplomatically. "Youth's enthusiasm sometimes overwhelms good sense."

"Speaking of good sense," the Dowager adjusted her lorgnette, "my son mentioned making your acquaintance last evening, Lady Ashworth. He was most impressed by your... astronomical interests."

Heat crept up Katherine's neck. Their conversation in that quiet hallway had wandered far from proper ballroom topics, touching on everything from celestial navigation to the latest scientific papers from the Royal Society. In those brief moments, she'd felt more herself than she had in years.

"The Earl was most kind," she managed. "Though I fear my amateur enthusiasm must have seemed quite provincial compared to his experiences abroad."

"Nonsense." The Dowager's eyes twinkled. "Marcus finds most society conversations tediously shallow. It's refreshing to meet someone who can discuss more than the weather and the latest on-dits."

"Mama is terribly clever," Charlotte interjected, a slight edge to her voice. "Though she hardly has time for such studies now, with my Season to manage."

The weight of maternal duty settled back onto Katherine's shoulders. Of course, Charlotte needed her full attention. These unexpected stirrings for Marcus Rutherford were nothing but middle-aged fancy.

Yet when the morning's stream of callers finally ebbed, Katherine found herself in her private study, running her fingers over the star charts hidden in her desk drawer. The numbers and calculations that had once been her sole passion now seemed to dance with new meaning, each constellation reminding her of the way Marcus's eyes had lit up when she'd mentioned her theories about stellar parallax.

How long has it been since anyone looked at me that way? Not as Charlotte's mother, not as the proper Viscountess Ashworth, but as simply Katherine—a woman with thoughts and dreams of her own. The memory of Marcus's intent expression as she explained her calculations made her fingers tremble against the desk drawer.

Stop this immediately. Her heart shouldn't race at the mere thought of how his large hand had briefly covered hers when she'd pointed out a particular constellation on her chart. She was hardly some green girl experiencing her first stirrings of attraction. She'd been married, for heaven's sake. Had borne a child. Had known the comfortable affection of a good marriage, if not the consuming passion that seemed to spark between her and Marcus with every shared glance.

James would understand. The thought came unbidden, bringing with it an image of her late husband's kind smile as he'd encouraged her to maintain her own interests even after Charlotte's birth. "A woman's mind doesn't stop working simply because she becomes a mother," he'd said. But James had been gone five years now, and in that time, she'd wrapped herself so thoroughly in maternal duty that she'd almost forgotten what it felt like to be seen as more than an extension of her daughter.

But Marcus sees me. The thought sent a shiver down her spine that had nothing to do with the morning room's pleasant temperature. He saw past the perfectly arranged copper curls and properly subdued widow's dress. When he'd quoted that passage from the latest Royal Society paper, his eyes had held a challenge, as if daring her to reveal the full breadth of her knowledge.

And heaven help me, I wanted to. She wanted to discuss theories that proper ladies shouldn't even know existed. Wanted to share the careful observations she'd recorded in her private journals. Wanted to...

Katherine pressed her palm flat against the desk, forcing her thoughts away from dangerous territory. *Charlotte needs me focused on her debut.* One wrong step now could ruin all their careful preparations. She couldn't risk her daughter's future happiness on these foolish stirrings of...

A knock at the door made her hastily shut the drawer. "Come in?"

Lord Timothy Ashworth entered, his familiar figure bringing both comfort and constraint. "Katherine, I hope I'm not interrupting?"

"Not at all." She gestured to a chair, noting how he chose to remain standing. "Is something troubling you?"

"I've heard... concerns." He shifted uncomfortably. "About Rutherford. His years in China... there are rumors."

"Surely you don't credit drawing room gossip?" Even as she spoke, Katherine felt a flicker of unease. *What did she really know about Marcus, beyond their one captivating conversation?*

"When it concerns my ward's future? I must consider every angle." Timothy's voice softened. "And those who might influence that future."

The gentle rebuke struck home. Katherine squared her shoulders, drawing her widow's dignity around her like armor. "You're right, of course. Charlotte's success must be our primary concern."

Yet later that afternoon, as she guided Charlotte through another round of social calls, Katherine couldn't quite suppress the thrill that ran through her when Marcus appeared in Lady Millicent's drawing room. Their eyes met across a sea of painted fans and nodding heads, and for one breathless moment, the weight of duty lifted from her shoulders.

Good heavens, how does he manage to fill a room so completely? The way Marcus held himself, with that quiet confidence born of years commanding his own ships—it drew the eye even among London's most polished gentlemen. His evening clothes might be impeccably tailored, but there was something untamed about him still, something that whispered of far horizons and adventures beyond the drawing room's confines.

Stop staring like a foolish schoolgirl. But her treacherous gaze kept finding him across the crowd, noting how the afternoon sun through Lady Millicent's windows caught the silver threading through his dark hair at the temples. How his large hands, more weathered than a typical peer's, handled the delicate teacup with surprising grace. How his eyes, when they met hers, held that same intense intelligence that had captivated her during their discussion of astronomical navigation.

This is precisely why widows must be more careful than debutantes. Every subtle glance, every shared look that lasted a heartbeat too long—it all meant so much more when one had the wisdom to understand what that heat in the blood could lead to. And Katherine understood all too well. Her marriage to James had been comfortable, affectionate, but it had never made her pulse race like this, never made her achingly aware of every inch of her skin.

I should leave now, before— But even as she formed the thought, Marcus shifted his position, angling himself so that when he appeared to be attending to Lady Constance's chatter, his gaze could rest unobserved on Katherine. The private smile that curved his lips, meant for her alone, sent warmth cascading through her body like fine brandy.

Lord give me strength. She needed every ounce of her hard-won social polish to maintain her composure. Yet beneath her serene expression, her mind raced with forbidden possibilities. *What would those weathered hands feel like against her skin? Would his kiss taste of adventure and foreign shores?* Would he...

Then Charlotte's voice cut through the moment, high and demanding, "Mama, Lady Constance says the silk flowers in my hair are quite passé. We must visit the modiste immediately!"

Katherine turned away from Marcus's gaze, back to her daughter's needs. But she could feel his eyes following her, burning with the same fierce intelligence that had drawn her in that first night. And somewhere deep inside, behind the perfect maternal mask she wore, an ember of rebellion began to glow.

. . .

L ater, in the safety of Mrs. Prudence Winters' back parlor, Katherine finally allowed her composure to crack. "I'm being utterly foolish," she confessed, pressing her fingers to her temples. "At my age, with my responsibilities..."

"At your age?" Prudence's laugh held the freedom of a woman who had already weathered society's storms. "My dear, you're barely eight and thirty, not eight and eighty. And from what I hear of Rutherford, he's hardly looking for some green girl fresh from the schoolroom."

"It doesn't matter what he's looking for." Katherine straightened her spine. "Charlotte needs—"

"Charlotte needs to see that her mother is a woman, not just an extension of her own desires." Prudence's voice gentled. "The girl's been the center of your world since James died. Perhaps it's time she learned to share."

Before Katherine could respond, the shop bell chimed. Through the beaded curtain, she glimpsed a familiar tall figure in the front room. Her heart leaped treacherously—then plummeted as Lady Constance Whitmore's voice rang out, clear and possessive: "My dear Lord Rutherford, how fortunate to encounter you here!"

Katherine gathered her reticule, mumbling excuses to Prudence. She slipped out through the back door and into the afternoon sunlight.

CHAPTER FIVE
A CHANCE IN THE PARK

The pre-dawn air held that peculiar London mixture of morning mist and coal smoke as Katherine guided her mare along Hyde Park's Rotten Row. At this hour, the fashionable riding path belonged only to early-rising servants and the occasional adventurous bluestocking who valued solitude over society's raised eyebrows.

Katherine adjusted her dark blue riding habit, grateful that the early hour meant no one would notice how last season's cut pulled a bit snugly across her shoulders. The sky had begun its slow transformation from pewter to pearl, perfect for observing the morning star that had occupied her calculations these past weeks. If she could just verify her measurements before the sun—

"Lady Ashworth?"

Her mare shied at the deep voice, or perhaps it was Katherine's own startled reaction that disturbed the animal. Either way, she found herself fighting for balance as Earl Rutherford appeared from a side path, his own mount a magnificent Arabian that made her reliable gelding seem decidedly provincial.

"My lord," Katherine's voice emerged remarkably steady, considering how her pulse had begun racing the moment she recognized him. "You're abroad early."

"Old habits from my seafaring days." He guided his horse alongside hers, close enough that their knees nearly touched. "Though I confess, I didn't expect to find anyone else appreciating Venus this morning."

Heat bloomed in her cheeks. "I'm sure I don't—"

"The morning star?" His grey eyes held that same intensity she remembered from their conversation at Almack's. "Unless I'm mistaken about the calculations I glimpsed in your hand?"

Katherine's fingers tightened on the small notebook she'd foolishly believed no one would notice. "You have sharp eyes, my lord."

"Among other useful qualities." The corner of his mouth lifted in a way that sent wholly inappropriate shivers down her spine. "Tell me, what do you make of Harrison's latest theory about using lunar distances for celestial navigation?"

The question caught her off guard – not because she couldn't answer it, but because she could. In detail. James had always nodded politely when she spoke of such things, his indulgent smile making it clear he considered it an amusing hobby, nothing more. But Marcus leaned forward in his saddle, one broad hand absently stroking his horse's neck as he waited for her response with genuine interest.

"I find his calculations regarding lunar parallax rather optimistic," she heard herself saying. "Particularly when one considers the practical difficulties of taking accurate measurements from a moving ship."

"Precisely!" His face lit with the kind of enthusiasm she usually reserved for private moments in her observatory. "The theoretical mathematics are sound enough, but at sea—" He launched into a detailed description of attempting such measurements during a storm off the coast of China.

Katherine found herself drawn into the discussion, her usual reserve melting away as they debated the relative merits of different navigational instruments. The sun rose higher, painting the park's trees in shades of gold, but neither of them seemed to notice the passing time. Their horses ambled along companionably as Marcus described the stars as seen from the deck of his ship in the South Seas, and Katherine shared her own observations about stellar movements.

Good heavens, I can't remember the last time I spoke so freely with anyone. The realization sent a flutter of something dangerously close to pleasure through Katherine's chest. The way Marcus leaned toward her as she described her theories, his grey eyes intent on her face—it made her feel as though her plain dark riding habit had transformed into something far more alluring.

Stop that this instant. She was a respectable widow, not some novel heroine about to lose her head over a handsome peer. Even if said peer's obvious intelligence made him far more appealing than the usual crop of society gentlemen. Even if the morning sunlight catching the silver at his temples made her fingers itch to discover if his hair felt as thick as it looked.

When did I become such a wanton? But there was something about the way he treated her calculations with genuine respect rather than indulgent tolerance. James had been kind about her astronomical interests, but he'd never truly understood them. Never debated the finer points of navigation with such passionate intensity that his horse drifted closer to hers with each point he made.

Lord help me, but I could talk with him forever. The thought should have shocked her propriety. Instead, she found herself noting how his large hands managed the reins with unconscious grace, wondering how those weathered fingers would feel against her skin. The morning air suddenly felt far too warm, despite her sensible riding costume.

What would it be like to share my observatory with someone who truly understands? Someone who saw the beauty in mathematics, who spoke of the stars as old friends rather than cold points of light. Someone who looked at her as though she were a fascinating puzzle he longed to solve.

Someone who makes me feel more alive than I have in years. The admission, even in the privacy of her own mind, sent heat blooming across her cheeks. She was Katherine Ashworth, pattern card of propriety, dedicated mother, sensible widow. She had no business entertaining such thoughts about a man who made her pulse race with nothing more dangerous than astronomical discussions.

"I have several star charts from my travels that might interest you," he said, his voice dropping to a lower register that seemed to vibrate through her bones. "Perhaps you might—"

"Mama!" Charlotte's voice shattered the morning's spell. "Mama, I've been looking everywhere for you!"

Katherine straightened in her saddle, reality crashing back as her daughter's riding party rounded the bend. Charlotte sat her horse with perfect grace, but the petulant set of her mouth suggested she'd noticed her mother's companion.

"Miss Charlotte," Marcus bowed from the saddle with elegant precision. "I trust you're enjoying your morning ride?"

"Oh, yes." Charlotte's smile didn't quite reach her eyes. "Though Mama usually joins my party rather than riding alone."

The hint of reproach in her daughter's voice made Katherine's spine stiffen. "I had some calculations to verify before—"

"Lady Ashworth! Miss Charlotte!" Lady Constance Whitmore's voice rang out across the morning air as she guided her perfectly matched grey mare toward their group. "How fortunate to encounter you here." Her smile encompassed them all, but her gaze lingered on Marcus with obvious intent. "My lord, I had no idea you were an early riser."

"There are many things about me that might surprise you, Lady Constance." The cool politeness in Marcus's voice contrasted sharply with the warmth he'd shown during their astronomical discussion.

A flurry of hoofbeats announced the arrival of the rest of Charlotte's riding party, accompanied by a thin man Katherine didn't recognize. His fashionable riding costume and perfectly arranged cravat marked him as a gentleman, but something in his sharp-eyed assessment of their group raised Katherine's hackles.

"Ah, cousin," Marcus's tone held a note of resignation. "Lady Ashworth, allow me to present Mr. Thomas Pembroke. Thomas, Lady Ashworth and her daughter, Miss Charlotte."

Katherine inclined her head politely, noting how Mr. Pembroke's gaze darted between her and Marcus with rather too much interest. The morning's gentle intimacy had shattered like sugar glass, leaving behind a sticky residue of social obligations and proper behavior.

"We really must be going," Katherine gathered her reins, ignoring the disappointment that flashed across Marcus's face. "Charlotte, your riding master will be waiting."

"But Mama—"

"Miss Charlotte speaks true," Lady Constance interjected smoothly. "A young lady shouldn't ride without proper companions. Lord Rutherford, surely you'll join our party? The morning is perfect for a gallop to the end of the Row."

Traffic from Bond Street had begun filtering into the park, bringing with it the usual parade of fashionable riders. Katherine watched Marcus's expression shift from the open enthusiasm of their private discussion to the polite mask of a society gentleman. The transformation left an odd ache in her chest.

Marcus watched Katherine guide her horse away, the elegant line of her back ramrod straight beneath her riding habit. *Damn and blast.* The morning's rare peace had shattered like a fine porcelain cup dropped on marble floors. His fingers tightened on his reins until the leather creaked in protest.

She's nothing like I expected. When his mother had first mentioned the widowed Viscountess Ashworth, he'd imagined yet another society matron focused solely on matrimonial schemes. Instead, he'd found a woman whose brilliant mind matched the fire in those remarkable green eyes. The way she'd analyzed Harrison's navigational theories with such precision, challenging his own assumptions...

Stop thinking about how her cheeks flushed when she grew passionate about stellar parallax. But the image persisted—Katherine's usual reserve melting away as she gestured animatedly, copper curls escaping their pins in the morning breeze. He'd wanted to brush those wayward strands back, to discover if her skin felt as soft as it looked.

This is madness. The ton expected him to seek a young bride, someone to give him an heir and oversee his household. Not a widow with a nearly-grown daughter and a mind that set his blood afire. Yet he couldn't forget how her eyes had lit up when he'd mentioned his star charts, or how her subtle curves had shifted in the saddle as she leaned closer to make a point about astronomical calculations.

Society would have a field day. He could already hear the whispers —the exotic Earl choosing a woman of eight and thirty, one who read scientific papers and calculated celestial movements like a university scholar. His mother would support them, he knew, but others would question his judgment. Question Katherine's motives.

Let them question. Twenty years commanding his own ships had taught him to trust his instincts. And every instinct he possessed told him that Katherine Ashworth was worth any amount of social censure. The way her mind worked, quick and precise as a ship's chronometer... the subtle wit beneath her proper façade... the glimpses of passion she tried so hard to hide...

Good God, I sound like a lovesick boy rather than a man of two and forty. But there was something about Katherine that made him feel young again, eager as a midshipman spotting his first foreign shore. He wanted to unlock all her hidden depths, to discover every secret that proper widow's mask concealed. To find out if her lips tasted as sweet as the smile she'd tried to suppress during their discussion of lunar tables.

She'll expect me to court her daughter. The thought was a bucket of cold seawater to his heated imagination. Society would certainly assume that was his aim—the wealthy Earl seeking a young bride, not falling hopelessly under the spell of her widowed mother. And Katherine herself... *would she even consider him? Or would she see only her duty to Charlotte?*

The morning sun had fully risen now, gilding the park's trees and turning Katherine's auburn hair to living flame as she rode away. Marcus watched until she disappeared around a bend, memorizing the graceful line of her throat, the subtle strength in her posture.

I'm in dangerous waters here. But then, he'd always preferred the excitement of uncharted seas to the safety of familiar harbors.

CHAPTER SIX
FAMILY TENSIONS

Katherine stared at the morning correspondence spread across her breakfast table, but the elegant script blurred before her eyes. The invitation to Rutherford House's musical evening lay innocently among the other papers, its cream-colored vellum somehow managing to dominate the entire array.

"Mama!" Charlotte's voice shattered the morning quiet as she swept into the breakfast room, still in her dressing gown despite the late hour. "My new silk flowers are completely wrong for the Merriweathers' ball. How could you possibly have approved such a shade of pink?"

The words barely registered as Katherine's fingers traced the edge of Marcus's invitation. His bold handwriting stood out against the page:

The Earl of Rutherford requests the pleasure of
Lady Ashworth's company

The formal words shouldn't have made her pulse quicken so treacherously.

"Mama, are you even listening?" Charlotte dropped into a chair with a dramatic sigh that set her brown curls bouncing. "Everyone will be at the Merriweathers' tonight, and my entire ensemble is ruined."

Katherine forced her attention away from the invitation. "The flowers are precisely the shade you selected at Madame Delafield's last week. You said they matched your complexion perfectly."

"That was before Lady Constance mentioned that pink flowers are completely passé. She says green is all the rage in Paris now." Charlotte's lower lip trembled. "You would know these things if you weren't so distracted lately."

The accusation struck uncomfortably close to home. Katherine had indeed been distracted – by memories of early morning rides and scientific discussions that made her feel more alive than she had in years.

Lord help me, but one look from him across a crowded ballroom undoes me completely. The memory of Marcus's hand at her waist during their waltz still burned through the layers of her evening gown hours after they'd parted. Such a proper dance, yet every turn had felt like an intimate caress.

I should not be thinking of his hands. But the image persisted— those strong, weathered fingers that had demonstrated navigational calculations in the air between them, that had brushed against hers when passing a teacup. *What would they feel like tangled in her hair, tracing the line of her throat, settling at her waist without layers of silk between them?*

Stop this immediately. Heat bloomed across her chest, and Katherine pressed her cool palms to her burning cheeks. She was a respectable widow, not some green girl mooning over her first suitor. Yet here she sat, haunted by the memory of Marcus's voice dropping to that low register that seemed to vibrate through her bones when he'd leaned close to whisper an observation about Lady Jersey's new turban.

I've become utterly foolish. But foolish or not, she couldn't stop remembering how the candlelight had caught the silver at his temples, how his eyes had darkened when she'd allowed a hint of her wit to show through her proper facade. The way his shoulders filled out his evening coat, the subtle scent of sandalwood that had enveloped her during their dance...

Just once, I'd like to touch him without gloves between us. The thought shocked her with its impropriety—and its intensity. She wanted to know if his skin was as warm as it looked, if those laugh lines at the corners of his eyes deepened when he smiled just for her, if his mouth tasted of the brandy he'd been drinking while he watched her across Lady Millicent's drawing room.

A discrete cough announced the arrival of Harrison, their butler. "Lord Timothy Ashworth, my lady."

Katherine straightened in her chair as her brother-in-law entered the breakfast room. His cravat was impeccably tied, his coat perfectly pressed, yet something in his expression set her nerves jangling.

"Katherine," he barely acknowledged Charlotte's presence with a nod. "I had hoped to catch you alone this morning. There are matters we must discuss."

"Surely they can wait until—"

"They cannot," Timothy's voice held an edge she'd never heard before. "It concerns certain... observations I've made recently. About the Earl of Rutherford's marked attention to our family."

Heat crept up Katherine's neck. "I'm sure I don't know what you mean."

"Don't you?" His eyes flickered to the invitation lying among her correspondence. "Three encounters at various drawing rooms this week alone. That rather infamous early morning ride in Hyde Park. And now a musical evening at his home?"

"Lord Rutherford has been perfectly correct in his behavior," Katherine said, proud of how steady her voice remained. "As the ton's most eligible peer, it's natural he would take an interest in this Season's debutantes."

Charlotte's head snapped up from her sulk. "Lord Rutherford has been paying attention to debutantes? But I haven't noticed him dancing with any—" She broke off, her eyes widening as she looked between her mother and uncle. "Oh."

The dawning comprehension in her daughter's face made Katherine's stomach clench. Before she could speak, Harrison appeared again.

"The morning's invitations, Miss Charlotte." He presented a small silver salver with several envelopes. "And Lady Sophia has arrived for your planned visit to the modiste."

Charlotte snatched up her correspondence, but her movements lacked their usual enthusiasm. Her gaze kept darting between Katherine and Timothy, calculation replacing her earlier petulance.

"We'll discuss this later," Timothy said as Charlotte reluctantly departed. The moment she was gone, he turned back to

Katherine. "You must see how this appears. A wealthy peer, recently returned from abroad, suddenly paying marked attention to a family with a marriageable daughter."

"Is that what concerns you?" Katherine kept her tone light. "That Marcus's intentions toward Charlotte might be improper?"

"Marcus, is it?" Timothy's jaw tightened. "And no, that is not what concerns me. What concerns me is watching my brother's widow risk her reputation – and by extension, Charlotte's future – on a man whose years in China have left him with a decidedly questionable understanding of proper behavior."

"I wasn't aware that discussing astronomical navigation qualified as improper behavior." The words emerged sharper than Katherine intended.

"No? Then perhaps you'd care to explain why Lady Jersey observed you and Rutherford in what she termed a 'most intense conversation' during Hartley's ball? Or why Lady Constance reports seeing you emerge from Mrs. Winters' shop mere moments after his departure?"

Each accusation landed like a physical blow. None of the encounters had been improper – indeed, they'd all occurred in public places with plenty of witnesses. But Timothy's recitation painted them in a light that made Katherine's cheeks burn.

"I am neither a green girl nor a fool," she said, forcing steel into her voice. "I am perfectly capable of managing both my reputation and my daughter's interests."

"Are you?" Timothy stepped closer, his voice dropping. "Because from where I stand, you appear to be risking everything James worked for – everything Charlotte deserves – on a man who spent the last twenty years consorting with foreign merchants rather than learning proper ton behavior."

"Lord Timothy?" Harrison's timing was impeccable as always. "Lord Pembroke has arrived with some urgent business papers requiring your attention."

Timothy's expression darkened. "This discussion isn't finished, Katherine."

But it was, at least for the moment. Katherine waited until both men had departed before allowing her rigid posture to relax. Her hands trembled slightly as she picked up Marcus's invitation again.

One dance. That's all it had taken at Hartley's ball – one perfectly proper waltz with the Earl, and already the ton's gossips were weaving their webs. She could still feel the warmth of his hand at her waist, the precise way he'd guided her through the steps while maintaining a perfectly acceptable distance between their bodies. Yet somehow that very correctness had made the dance more intimate than any improper embrace.

"Mama?" Charlotte stood in the doorway, her blue eyes shrewd in a way that made her look startlingly adult. "Was Uncle Timothy speaking about Lord Rutherford's interest in... me?"

Katherine's heart plummeted as she stared at her daughter's calculating expression. The question hung between them like a tangible thing, forcing her to confront the very possibility she'd been avoiding.

Was he? Had Marcus's attention been directed toward Charlotte all along? The thought created a sickening hollowness in her chest.

"I..." Katherine's throat felt tight. She reached for her teacup, buying precious seconds to compose herself. "Lord Rutherford's interests are his own affair."

"But Uncle Timothy seemed quite concerned about his attention to our family," Charlotte drifted closer, her movements carrying that new awareness that made Katherine's nerves prickle. "And Lady Constance did mention that he's seeking a wife."

Of course, Lady Constance would have mentioned that. The woman never missed an opportunity to remind the ton that Marcus remained unwed. Katherine's fingers tightened around the delicate porcelain.

"Many gentlemen of the ton are seeking wives." The words tasted bitter. "That's the very purpose of the Season."

"True," Charlotte settled into the chair opposite, smoothing her skirts with deliberate care. "Though most of them aren't wealthy Earls who've spent years in exotic lands. Lady Jersey says his fortune is simply enormous."

Katherine's stomach twisted. The thought of Marcus courting Charlotte was somehow worse than imagining him with Lady Constance or any other woman. Her own daughter. The very idea felt wrong, like a discordant note in an otherwise perfect symphony.

"He's far too old for you," Katherine blurted, then immediately wished she could recall the words.

Charlotte's eyebrows rose. "The Duke of Montgomery is forty-five, and he's courting Miss Edwards who only just turned eighteen." Her head tilted. "Lord Rutherford cannot be more than forty-two or three. And he's quite handsome, in a distinguished way."

Distinguished. Yes, that was precisely the word for the silver threading his temples and the laugh lines that crinkled when he smiled. But those smiles weren't meant for Charlotte - were they? They'd been directed at Katherine, hadn't they?

"Besides," Charlotte continued, "he's clearly interested in our family. Why else would he keep appearing everywhere we go?"

Because he shared Katherine's passion for astronomy. Because he understood what it meant to feel trapped by society's expectations. Because when he looked at her, Katherine felt seen for the first time in years.

But she couldn't say any of that.

"I hardly think—" Katherine's voice emerged strangled. She cleared her throat and tried again. "Lord Rutherford's attention to our family has been nothing more than common courtesy."

"If you say so, Mama," Charlotte rose, brushing imaginary crumbs from her skirts. "Though I must say, he does have the most interesting way of showing courtesy. I don't recall him discussing the proper alignment of stars with any other lady's mama."

The observation struck too close to home. Katherine's hands trembled as she set down her tea cup. "Shouldn't you be meeting Lady Sophia?"

"Oh yes, the modiste," Charlotte paused at the doorway. "Though perhaps I should pay more attention to green trimmings than pink, if I'm to catch an Earl's eye."

The door closed behind her daughter with a decisive click, leaving Katherine alone with her churning thoughts. The mere idea of Marcus courting Charlotte made her physically ill. He wouldn't—surely he wouldn't consider someone so young, so untested by life?

But why wouldn't he? Every other peer seemed to seek out the youngest, freshest debutantes. And Charlotte was beautiful, well-dowered, and impeccably connected. On paper, she would make an excellent countess.

Katherine pressed her palms against her burning cheeks. *How had she allowed herself to indulge in such foolish fantasies?* Of course Marcus's attention to their family centered on Charlotte. It would be absurd to think otherwise. She was a widow of eight-and-thirty, past her prime, while Charlotte represented everything the ton valued - youth, beauty, and malleability.

The invitation to his musical evening suddenly felt like it was burning through the table. Katherine wanted nothing more than to cry off, to avoid watching him pay court to her daughter. But that would only confirm the rumors already circulating about her inappropriate interest in the Earl.

No, she would have to attend. Would have to smile and make pleasant conversation while watching Marcus's attention shift inevitably toward Charlotte. Would have to pretend her heart wasn't splintering at the very thought.

What a fool she'd been, imagining those shared moments meant anything more than polite interest in his future mother-in-law.

CHAPTER SEVEN

DRESSING EXPECTATIONS

Katherine wove through the chaos of Charlotte's chambers, navigating between scattered silk ribbons and discarded accessories. Her daughter's preparations for the evening's ball had transformed the elegant room into a battleground of fashion, with gowns draped across chairs and hairpins scattered like fallen soldiers across the vanity.

"Hold still, darling," Katherine adjusted the ivory satin of Charlotte's gown, smoothing a rebellious ruffle. "Charlotte, have you considered your options for this evening? I suppose you would have some favorites in mind?"

Charlotte barely acknowledged her mother's query, lost in her reflection as she tilted her head this way and that, examining the placement of each brunette curl.

Katherine pressed her lips together, then ventured forth. "I must admit, I've seen how you look at Lord Pembroke. Is he already the object of your affections?"

Charlotte spun around, her skirts swishing across the carpet. A coy smile played at her lips. "Mama, surely there are more compelling gentlemen than a man returned from the seas. What of Captain Lark? Or Mr. Ellis with his charming smile?"

"Oh, but Captain Lark is known for his volatile temper, and I understand Mr. Ellis's family is in rather poor standing." Katherine met her daughter's gaze in the mirror, willing her to understand the subtle warning.

"There's Lord Fairchild," Katherine continued, adjusting a wayward curl. "I hear he has an impressive estate and might be just the gentleman to sweep you off your feet."

Charlotte's reflection showed her dramatic eye roll. "But he's rather dull, isn't he?"

"Dull? Or perhaps just steady?" Katherine's fingers stilled in Charlotte's hair. "Not every man requires the charm of a dancing peacock."

Charlotte's face clouded with frustration as she reached for her pearl-handled brush, attacking an already perfect curl with unnecessary vigor.

"What if, just this once, you put aside your whims?" Katherine caught her daughter's hand, stilling its motion. "There are other gentlemen who would be a better match for your future."

The defiance in Charlotte's expression softened, just slightly, as she lowered the brush. "But what if I want something more than just a good match? Is it so wrong to dream of a more exciting life, like love?"

Katherine's chest tightened as she studied Charlotte's pleading expression. How familiar that yearning looked - she had worn the same desperate hope at eighteen, standing in her father's study as he announced her betrothal to James Ashworth, Viscount Blackwood.

"Your mother and I have arranged an excellent match," her father had declared, his satisfaction evident in the way he rocked back on his heels. "The Viscount is looking for a wife of good breeding and proper deportment. You'll do very well."

The memory of that moment still stung, even now. Katherine had gripped her hands together so tightly her knuckles had gone white, fighting back the urge to protest. A Baron's daughter had no right to refuse such an advantageous match. Her mother had drilled that lesson into her since childhood—their family's elevation depended on strategic alliances.

"The wedding will take place in three months," her father had continued, already turning back to his ledgers. "Your mother will see to the preparations."

Katherine's fingers traced the delicate lace at Charlotte's sleeve, remembering how she had stood silent and trembling before her own mirror on her wedding day. The Viscount had been kind enough, in his way. Proper. Correct. Everything a nobleman should be—except in love with his bride.

Those first years had been the hardest. Night after night, lying beside a virtual stranger, both of them too proper to breach the careful distance between them. She had tried so hard to be the perfect viscountess, to make him proud, to earn if not his love then at least his regard.

Love had come eventually, creeping in so slowly she barely noticed its arrival. Small moments—his hand steadying her elbow as she descended the stairs, the way he would save particularly amusing passages from his reading to share with her over breakfast, his quiet pride when she managed the household accounts with precision.

But by then, illness had already begun stealing him away. Their hard-won affection had made his passing all the more bitter. Katherine could still recall the ache of watching him fade, knowing they had wasted so many years maintaining proper distance when they might have had so much more.

"Mama?" Charlotte's voice drew Katherine back to the present. Her daughter was watching her with an unusual perception. "You're thinking of Papa again, aren't you?"

Katherine smoothed her features into a careful smile. "I was thinking of when I was your age. And how certain I was that I knew exactly what I wanted from life."

"Did you want love too?" Charlotte's question held none of her usual petulance.

"I did," Katherine adjusted the drape of Charlotte's shawl, buying time to steady her voice. "But I did not understand then that love takes many forms. Your father and I... we found our way to it eventually. Though perhaps not in the way I'd imagined as a girl."

Charlotte turned back to the mirror, but her reflection showed thoughtfulness rather than vanity. "Was it very difficult? Being married to someone you did not love at first?"

"It was..." Katherine paused, choosing her words carefully. "Lonely. For both of us, I think. We were so concerned with being proper, with meeting expectations, that we forgot to simply be kind to each other."

The admission cost her something to voice aloud. She had never spoken of this to Charlotte before, had maintained the fiction of a perfect marriage even after James's death. But perhaps her daughter needed to understand that love wasn't always a lightning strike, that sometimes it grew in the quiet spaces between duty and desire.

Charlotte's fingers worried at the edge of her shawl. "But you did love him, in the end?"

"Yes," Katherine's throat tightened around the word. "Though I sometimes wonder if we might have found happiness sooner had we both been braver, less concerned with what was proper, and more willing to be vulnerable." Katherine released a careful breath, "Just promise me, dear, to keep your heart open to all gentlemen. The right one might surprise you, and he needn't bear the title of Earl."

Their eyes met in the mirror's reflection, and Katherine squeezed her daughter's shoulder before reaching for the pearl necklace that would complete her ensemble. As she fastened the clasp, her fingers brushed against Charlotte's neck, warm and alive with youth's endless possibilities.

Katherine offered her hand to help Charlotte rise from her seat. Their gazes held for a moment longer, weighted with unspoken thoughts before they turned toward the door together.

Charlotte's fingers caught her mother's sleeve just as they reached the door. "Mama, wait," her voice held an unusual tremor. "There's something I need to tell you."

Katherine turned, studying her daughter's face. The carefully arranged mask of societal politeness had slipped, revealing a glimpse of genuine uncertainty beneath.

"I..." Charlotte's fingers twisted in her skirts. "There are two gentlemen I've been thinking of. Mr. Carmichael—"

"The tradesman's son?" Katherine's eyebrows rose.

"He has the most wonderful way of speaking about art. Did you know he's traveled to Italy? And his father's business has made him quite wealthy." A blush crept across Charlotte's cheeks. "But then there's Lord Ridlington."

Katherine's chest tightened at the mention of the young lord who had already disappointed her daughter twice. "My dear—"

"I know what you're going to say." Charlotte lifted her chin. "That he's proven unreliable. That his excuse of a hunting accident the first time and his grandmother's sudden illness the second were convenient falsehoods. But when he does appear at events, he's so charming."

"Charm can mask a multitude of deficiencies in character," Katherine said softly.

Charlotte's shoulders slumped. "I suppose you're right. But at least they're both of an age with me." She straightened, a hint of her usual spirit returning. "Unlike Lord Pembroke."

Katherine's hand stilled on the doorknob. "Lord Pembroke?"

"Oh, I've noticed how he watches at events. It's rather thrilling to have caught the eye of someone so distinguished." Charlotte's laugh held a note of dismissal. "But really, Mama, he must be ancient. At least forty! I could never imagine falling in love with someone so..." She waved her hand vaguely. "Mature."

Katherine forced her features to remain neutral, though something in her chest constricted at her daughter's casual dismissal. "Age often brings wisdom and steadiness of character."

"Perhaps." Charlotte smoothed her skirts. "But I want romance, Mama. Adventure. Not some stuffy old Earl who probably spends his evenings reading shipping ledgers." She patted her mother's arm. "Though I suppose he might make a fine match for someone more... settled."

The words hung in the air between them, Charlotte clearly oblivious to how they might cut. Katherine drew in a careful breath, reminding herself that at eighteen, anyone over thirty might as well be ancient.

"Well," Katherine managed, her voice steady despite the sudden hollow feeling in her chest. "We should join the others. Your aunt will be wondering what's delayed us."

Charlotte nodded, already distracted by one final check of her reflection. "Do you think Mr. Carmichael will be at Lady Whitmore's tonight?"

"I believe his family received an invitation." Katherine opened the door, gesturing for Charlotte to precede her.

"Excellent." Charlotte swept past, her earlier vulnerability replaced by her usual confident demeanor. "And Lord Ridlington simply must attend. After all, he does owe me at least one dance."

Katherine followed her daughter into the hallway, their heels clicking against the polished floor in perfect synchronization. She told herself the ache in her chest was merely a concern for Charlotte's romantic notions. Nothing more.

Katherine's mind whirled with possibilities as they descended the grand staircase, her fingers trailing along the polished mahogany banister. Charlotte's confession about her two potential suitors had sparked an idea - one that might help guide her daughter toward a more suitable match while steering her away from inappropriate choices.

"I was thinking," Katherine kept her tone light as they reached the landing, "perhaps we might arrange a small gathering in the gardens next week. The weather has been particularly fine."

Charlotte paused mid-step, her face brightening. "Oh! Would you really? Lady Whitmore's garden parties are always so tedious - all those ancient dowagers clustered around the tea tables."

"I thought we might invite a select group." Katherine watched her daughter's reaction carefully. "The Carmichaels, for instance. I hear young Mr. Carmichael has quite progressive ideas about landscape design."

"His thoughts on Italian gardens are fascinating." Charlotte's cheeks colored slightly. "Though I suppose we'd have to invite Lord Ridlington as well, to maintain proper balance."

"Naturally." Katherine gestured for Charlotte to continue down the stairs. "We wouldn't want anyone to suspect particular attention to any one gentleman."

Charlotte's steps quickened with enthusiasm. "We could have music! And perhaps some poetry readings. Mr. Carmichael does recite beautifully."

"If Lord Ridlington attends," Katherine couldn't resist adding.

Charlotte's smile faltered slightly. "Yes, well, he's been rather occupied lately. His grandmother's health, you understand."

"Of course." Katherine kept her skepticism from her voice. "Though one might think a truly interested gentleman would find time for social obligations, despite family concerns."

They reached the bottom of the stairs, where Thompson waited with their pelisses. As the butler helped them with their wraps, Katherine continued planning.

"I shall write to both families this evening. Nothing too formal - merely a pleasant afternoon gathering with a select group of friends."

Charlotte fidgeted with her gloves. "Do you really think Lord Ridlington will come?"

"His response will tell us much about his character, won't it?" Katherine adjusted her daughter's shawl. "As will Mr. Carmichael's."

The carriage waited outside, gleaming in the late afternoon sun. As they settled onto the plush seats, Katherine reached for her daughter's hand.

"Sometimes the best way to understand a gentleman's intentions is to observe him in a more intimate setting. Away from the pressure of formal balls and public scrutiny."

Charlotte squeezed her fingers. "You're quite clever, Mama."

"I've had some experience in these matters." Katherine smiled, already composing the letters in her head. She would write them tonight - careful, elegant invitations that would reveal volumes in their responses.

The carriage pulled away from the curb, and Katherine gazed out the window at the passing houses. Yes, she would arrange this gathering with meticulous care. It was time to separate the wheat from the chaff, to see which of these young men might truly be worthy of her daughter's attention.

And if Lord Ridlington proved as unreliable as she suspected, well - perhaps Mr. Carmichael's foreign travels and artistic sensibilities would provide a more stable foundation for Charlotte's romantic notions. After all, Katherine reflected, true love often grew from shared interests rather than mere surface charm.

She would word the invitations perfectly - subtle enough to avoid any hint of matchmaking, yet clear enough to demand a response. The gardens would be arranged just so, with quiet corners for conversation and open areas for general mingling. She would invite just enough other guests to provide proper chaperonage without overwhelming the intimate atmosphere.

And then she would watch. Watch how Mr. Carmichael engaged with the other guests. Watch whether Lord Ridlington could be bothered to attend. Watch her daughter's reactions to both gentlemen when they weren't performing for a ballroom audience.

Yes, Katherine decided as their carriage joined the evening traffic. She would write those letters tonight, and set in motion events that might well determine her daughter's future happiness.

QUIET EXPECTATIONS

T he British Museum's Egyptian Hall stood silent in the early morning light, dust motes dancing through the air like tiny stars. Katherine traced her fingers along the edge of a glass case, pretending to study the ancient artifacts while her mind whirled with calculations from her latest astronomical observations. Here, among the remnants of past civilizations, she could drop the mask of the perfect society widow for a few precious moments.

The sound of footsteps echoing on marble made her stiffen, ready to assume her proper social facade. But when she turned, it was the Earl Rutherford standing in the doorway, his broad shoulders blocking the morning light.

"I thought I might find you here," he said quietly, crossing the space between them with that fluid grace that made her pulse quicken. "Lady Millicent mentioned your interest in Egyptian mathematics."

"Did she?" Katherine's fingers clenched around her small notebook. "Or perhaps you noticed my carriage outside?"

A smile tugged at the corner of his mouth. "I may have observed it while passing by. Pure coincidence, of course."

"Of course." But she couldn't quite suppress an answering smile. In the filtered light, his grey eyes held a warmth that made her skin tingle. "Though I wonder what brings the Earl Rutherford to the museum so early in the morning?"

"The same thing that brings you, I'd wager." He moved closer, ostensibly to examine the hieroglyphics she'd been studying. The scent of sandalwood enveloped her. "A desire for intellectual pursuits without society's constant observation."

His shoulder brushed hers as he leaned in to inspect the ancient numbers. Katherine held herself perfectly still, acutely aware of every point where their bodies nearly touched. "The Egyptians had quite sophisticated astronomical calculations," she managed.

"Indeed," his voice dropped lower, meant for her ears alone. "Though I suspect your own calculations regarding stellar parallax might surprise them. May I?" He gestured to her notebook.

Katherine hesitated only a moment before holding it out. Their fingers brushed during the exchange, sending sparks of awareness shooting up her arm. Marcus's large hands made the small book appear delicate as he carefully turned the pages, studying her neat columns of numbers and precise observations.

"Remarkable," he murmured. "You've accounted for variables I've never considered. This could revolutionize navigation calculations."

"You're laughing at me."

"Never." The intensity in his gaze pinned her in place. "Katherine, these calculations are brilliant. They deserve to be published in the Royal Society's papers."

The use of her given name should have shocked her. Instead, it sent a shiver of pleasure down her spine. "A woman publishing scientific papers? The ton would have apoplexy."

"The ton," Marcus said with quiet conviction, "does not deserve you."

Katherine's breath caught as Marcus's grey eyes held hers, the intensity in them making her forget they stood in a public gallery. *Had he always been standing quite so close?* She could count the silver threads at his temples, see the tiny laugh lines that crinkled at the corners of his eyes when they shared private jokes about astronomical calculations.

Good Lord, I'm staring at his mouth. Heat crept up her neck as she forced her gaze away from his lips, but that was hardly better. His cravat was slightly askew – just enough to reveal a tantalizing glimpse of his throat, making her fingers itch to straighten the fine linen. Or perhaps to muss it further.

Stop that this instant. Yet she couldn't help noticing how his large hands still cradled her notebook, his thumbs brushing the pages where her midnight calculations were recorded. Such careful strength in those weathered fingers. *What would they feel like against her skin, tracing the same patterns he'd drawn in the air while describing constellation movements?*

Anyone could walk in at any moment. The thought should have made her step back, resume a proper distance. Instead, she found herself swaying slightly closer, drawn by the subtle scent of sandalwood and male warmth. One step more and her skirts would brush his boots. One slight lean forward and she could feel if his coat was as soft as it looked.

I've gone utterly mad. Her heart thundered so loudly she was certain he must hear it echoing off the marble walls. She should look away from the heat in his eyes, the way his pupils had dilated until only a thin ring of grey remained. But her body seemed to have developed a will of its own, every inch of her skin achingly aware of his proximity.

Just once, I'd like to... The thought trailed off as his tongue darted out to wet his lower lip. Such a tiny movement, yet it sent liquid heat pooling in her belly. *What would he taste like if she closed that last inch between them? Would his mouth be as warm as the hands that still held her notebook as carefully as if it were a precious treasure?*

Before Katherine could respond, voices echoed from the adjoining hall—young, feminine voices that included Charlotte's unmistakable tones. Reality crashed back like a wave breaking over a ship's bow.

Marcus stepped back smoothly, assuming a proper distance just as Charlotte appeared with several other young ladies. Her eyes narrowed at the sight of her mother standing close to the exotic Earl.

Marcus cleared his throat, fighting the near-overwhelming urge to reach for Katherine. *Dear God, does she have any idea what she does to me?* Standing this close, he could see the subtle amber flecks in her green eyes, count each delicate freckle that powdered her nose despite her careful use of parasols.

Control yourself, man. You commanded ships through typhoons, surely you can master this. But watching Katherine's fingers trace those ancient hieroglyphics had been pure torment. Such elegant hands—a scholar's hands, an artist's hands. He imagined them trailing across his chest, tangling in his hair, drawing him closer for a kiss that would shock the ton's sensibilities.

Stop thinking about her mouth. Yet his gaze kept dropping to her lips as she spoke about Egyptian mathematics. Such a proper topic of conversation, but the passion in her voice when she discussed calculations made his blood heat. *What would that passion taste like? Would she gasp if he backed her against the glass case and showed her exactly how much her brilliant mind aroused him?*

Twenty years at sea, and I'm undone by one widow's smile. The morning light catching her copper curls wasn't helping his composure. One tendril had escaped its pins, brushing her elegant neck in a way that made his fingers itch to follow its path. He wanted to undo every proper pin, watch that glorious hair cascade over his pillows while he explored every inch of her.

She deserves to be worshipped, not pawed at like some dockside fancy. The thought steadied him, barely. The Viscountess was a lady, not some casual dalliance. She deserved elaborate courtship, proper negotiations, every social nicety that would protect her reputation. Not to be compromised in a museum gallery by a man who could barely keep his hands from shaking with the need to touch her.

"Mama! I did not know you planned to visit the museum this morning." Charlotte's smile held a brittle edge. "Lady Sophia and I are showing Miss Carrington the Egyptian antiquities."

"Lord Rutherford was just explaining some fascinating details about ancient mathematics," Katherine said smoothly, hating how quickly she'd reverted to her social mask. "The Egyptians' understanding of astronomical calculations was quite advanced."

"How thrilling," Charlotte said in a tone that suggested it was anything but. "Though I'm sure Lord Rutherford has more pressing engagements than discussing old numbers with—"

"Your mother's insights are invaluable," Marcus interrupted, his voice carrying that subtle note of command that never failed to make Katherine's breath catch. "Her understanding of celestial navigation rivals any scholar's."

Charlotte's eyes widened at his defense, then narrowed again as she glanced between them. The other young ladies tittered behind their fans, and Katherine could already hear the gossip spreading through the ton's drawing rooms.

"Miss Charlotte," Lady Sophia stepped forward, revealing the social awareness that made her such a good influence on Katherine's daughter. "Weren't you eager to show Miss Carrington the new Roman sculptures? I believe they're in the west wing."

Katherine watched Charlotte's group disappear around the corner, their laughter echoing off the museum's marble walls. The weight of duty pressed against her chest, urging her to follow. But before she could take a step, Marcus's hand brushed her elbow, the touch whisper-soft through her silk sleeve.

"Stay," he murmured, his voice pitched low enough that even the ever-present museum attendants couldn't hear. "Just for a moment."

Katherine's pulse quickened. She ought to move away, maintain the proper distance that society—and her role as Charlotte's mother—demanded. Instead, she remained still, achingly aware of his presence behind her.

"Being near you," Marcus said, each word measured as carefully as his astronomical calculations, "brings me a joy I had not thought to find in England."

The admission stole her breath. Katherine turned, needing to see his face, to read the truth in those storm-grey eyes. "I—" The word caught in her throat as their gazes met. "I feel it too."

Marcus's eyes dropped to her lips, and the air between them grew thick with possibility. He swayed forward, just slightly, and Katherine's heart thundered against her ribs. But then voices echoed from the adjacent gallery—Charlotte's voice among them—and the moment shattered like fine crystal.

Marcus straightened, his expression shifting from yearning to careful neutrality with practiced ease. Yet his eyes, when they met hers again, held promises that made her shiver despite the warmth of the afternoon sun streaming through the museum's windows.

"Until tonight's assembly, Lady Ashworth," he said, offering a perfectly proper bow.

Katherine managed a curtsey, though her knees felt oddly weak. "My lord."

She watched him stride away, his broad shoulders straight with military precision and pressed her hand to her chest where her heart still raced beneath layers of silk and propriety. This attraction to Marcus was becoming increasingly difficult to ignore—and increasingly dangerous to indulge.

With a steadying breath, she turned to follow the sound of her daughter's voice, knowing that duty must triumph over desire. But the phantom warmth of his touch lingered on her elbow, a sweet torment she would carry with her for the rest of the day.

Charlotte rounded the corner of the Egyptian gallery with Lady Sophia and Miss Carrington, their slippers whispering against the marble floor. The sound of male laughter brought them to an abrupt halt. Three gentlemen stood clustered around a weathered statue of Aphrodite, their morning coats a stark contrast against the pale stone.

Her breath caught as she recognized Mr. Albert Carmichael among them. The morning light from the high windows caught the golden highlights in his artfully tousled hair as he gestured animatedly, describing something that had his companions in stitches.

"I tell you, the horse nearly threw me directly into the fountain," Albert was saying. He turned at the sound of their approach, his bright blue eyes lighting up. "Ah, ladies! You've arrived just in time to save my reputation. Surely you don't believe I would be so clumsy?"

"I wouldn't dare venture an opinion, Mr. Carmichael," Lady Sophia replied with a demure smile that made something twist in Charlotte's stomach. "Though I have heard tales of your adventures in Hyde Park."

Albert pressed a hand to his chest in mock outrage. "You wound me, Lady Sophia. And here I thought we were friends." His gaze slid to Charlotte, but she kept her eyes firmly fixed on the statue's face.

"Friends who tell tales out of school, perhaps," Lady Sophia teased, and Charlotte had never heard that playful note in her friend's voice before.

"Then I must insist you allow me to defend myself properly at tonight's assembly," Albert said, taking a step closer to Sophia. "The first waltz, perhaps?"

Charlotte's fingers tightened on her fan. *Why should it matter if Albert wanted to dance with Sophia? After all, Lord Ridlington would be at the assembly as well, and he was far more suitable. More mature. More... everything.*

"I believe my dance card may have an opening," Sophia replied with perfect composure, though a becoming blush stained her cheeks.

"May have?" Albert raised an eyebrow. "I shall have to arrive early to ensure no other gentleman claims that spot."

Miss Carrington giggled behind her fan, and Charlotte suddenly couldn't bear another moment of watching Albert's attention focused so intently on her best friend. "We should continue our tour," she said, proud of how steady her voice remained. "Mama will wonder where we've gone."

"Of course," Sophia agreed immediately, ever aware of social propriety. "Good morning, gentlemen."

As they moved past the group, Albert bowed with a flourish. "Until tonight, Lady Sophia." His eyes met Charlotte's for just a moment, something unreadable in their depths before he turned back to Sophia with another brilliant smile.

Charlotte led their small group around the next corner perhaps more quickly than strictly necessary, her thoughts in a whirl. *Why should Albert's flirtation with Sophia bother her?* He was merely one of many gentlemen paying court during the Season. She had certainly noticed his charm before, but until this moment, she'd considered him little more than an amusing distraction.

And yet... the memory of his smile directed at Sophia made her chest feel oddly tight. It was the same smile he'd worn while teaching her the new quadrille steps at Lady Jersey's ball last week. The same warmth in his voice when he'd complimented her playing at the musical evening.

"Charlotte?" Sophia touched her arm gently. "Are you well? You seem distracted."

"Perfectly well," Charlotte replied, forcing a bright smile. "I was just thinking about tonight's assembly. Lord Ridlington promised to dance the first set with me, you know."

But even as she spoke the words, she wondered why the thought of Lord Ridlington's serious grey eyes and proper manners didn't spark the same flutter in her stomach as Albert's laughing blue ones. It made no sense. Lord Ridlington was exactly the sort of match her mother would approve of. The sort of match she should want.

The girls continued their tour of the museum, but Charlotte found herself unable to focus on Miss Carrington's chatter about the Roman artifacts. Instead, her thoughts kept returning to the way Albert's eyes had lingered on Sophia's face, the teasing lilt in his voice as he secured his dance.

She should be planning how to capture Lord Ridlington's attention at tonight's assembly. Instead, she was wondering if Albert would seek out Sophia for more than just that first waltz, and why that possibility made her want to tear her carefully arranged curls out of their pins.

CHAPTER NINE
WEATHER OR NOT

The leaden sky had threatened rain all morning, but Katherine had insisted on walking the short distance to her modiste, desperate for a moment of solitude after Charlotte's increasingly demanding behavior. Now, as the first heavy drops pelted the cobblestones of Berkeley Square, she realized her stubbornness would cost her both her dignity and her new morning dress.

Katherine quickened her pace as another raindrop struck her bonnet, her thoughts as turbulent as the darkening sky above. The morning's quarrel with Charlotte still rang in her ears—yet another battle in what felt like an endless war of wills.

"But Mama, Lord Ridlington promised he would be there!" Charlotte had wailed over breakfast, picking at her toast with the sort of dramatic despair only the young could muster. "How dare he send his regrets at the last possible moment?"

The memory of Charlotte's subsequent tantrum made Katherine's temples throb. She had attempted to explain, with all the patience she could gather, that Lord Ridlington's absence likely stemmed from his grandmother's declining health—a perfectly reasonable excuse that any well-bred young lady should understand.

"I care not for his excuses," Charlotte had declared, throwing down her napkin. "If he truly wished to court me, he would find a way to attend. And did you see how Mr. Carmichael swooped in the moment we were leaving? As if he had been waiting in the shadows!"

Katherine's lips pressed into a thin line at the recollection. Indeed, Albert Carmichael's timing had been suspiciously perfect, appearing just as they descended the steps of Lady Whitmore's townhouse. The way he had materialized beside their carriage, all charm and gleaming smiles, spoke of careful calculation rather than chance.

"Miss Ashworth," he had crooned, catching Charlotte's gloved hand. "Surely you cannot be departing so soon? The evening has barely begun."

Katherine had watched, stomach clenching, as her daughter transformed from sulking child to sparkling debutante in the space of a heartbeat. Charlotte's practiced laugh had tinkled through the evening air like crystal bells.

"Oh, Mr. Carmichael, you know how these things can be. One must leave them wanting more."

The memory of Charlotte's coquettish glance made Katherine's chest tight. She had tried, Lord knew she had tried, to instill some sense of propriety in her daughter. "A lady never appears too eager," she had counseled that very morning. "Nor does she publicly bemoan a gentleman's absence, no matter how keenly she feels it."

Charlotte had merely tossed her brunette curls. "Times are changing, Mama. We needn't be bound by such rigid rules anymore."

A particularly fat raindrop landed on Katherine's cheek, and she brushed it away with more force than necessary. The rigid rules, as Charlotte so dismissively called them, were what kept young ladies from scandal and ruin. They were what separated the truly elegant from the merely fashionable.

But how could she make Charlotte understand? The girl lived in a world of her own making, where every wish was granted, every whim indulged. Katherine's own past efforts at protecting her daughter from pain had created this creature who saw no reason why the world should not bend to her desires.

Last night's early departure had been necessary—Charlotte's loud complaints about Lord Ridlington had begun drawing attention from precisely the wrong sort of people. Lady Jersey's raised eyebrow alone had been enough to send Katherine into a panic.

"We simply cannot stay, my dear," she had whispered urgently to her daughter. "You are making yourself conspicuous in all the wrong ways."

Charlotte had gone, but not without a performance worthy of Drury Lane. And then Mr. Carmichael's perfectly timed appearance - as if he had been waiting for just such an opportunity to present himself as a consolation prize.

Katherine could still see the calculating gleam in his eye as he'd helped Charlotte into the carriage, the way his hand lingered a fraction too long on her daughter's arm. The boy was hunting for a wealthy wife, that much was clear. And Charlotte, in her current state of pique over Lord Ridlington's absence, was precisely the sort of prey he sought.

The rain began to fall in earnest now, and Katherine quickened her steps further. She had failed this morning—failed to make Charlotte understand the delicate balance required in society, failed to curb her daughter's increasingly willful behavior. The argument had ended as so many did these days, with Charlotte sweeping from the room in a rustle of muslin and wounded pride, leaving Katherine alone with her fears and regrets.

Lightning split the sky, followed by a crash of thunder that made her jump. The few other pedestrians scattered, ducking into shops or beneath awnings, leaving Katherine alone in the growing deluge. She quickened her pace, lifting her skirts above the rapidly forming puddles.

"Lady Ashworth!"

The deep voice cut through the drumming rain. Katherine turned to find Marcus striding toward her, his own coat already darkening with moisture.

"You must take shelter," he called, closing the distance between them in long steps. "Rutherford House is just there."

Another crack of thunder punctuated his words. Katherine hesitated, calculating the propriety of accepting versus the certainty of ruination—either of her reputation if seen entering his home unchaperoned, or of her clothing if she attempted to reach Ashworth House in this downpour.

"I assure you Mrs. Fletcher is at home," Marcus added, reading her hesitation. "And my mother often calls at this hour."

A particularly vicious gust of wind decided for her, driving icy rain beneath her bonnet. Katherine nodded, allowing Marcus to guide her toward the imposing townhouse. His hand at her elbow burned through the wet fabric of her sleeve, sending warmth spreading despite the chill.

The butler opened the door before they reached it, and Katherine found herself ushered into the marble-floored entrance hall. Water pooled beneath their feet as Marcus helped her remove her sodden pelisse.

"Bring hot tea to my study," he instructed the hovering servant. "And send Mrs. Fletcher down immediately."

Katherine knew she should protest being led to his private domain, but curiosity warred with propriety. She had glimpsed this room only once before, during a formal tour given by the Dowager Countess. Now, with rain lashing the windows and thunder rolling overhead, it felt like entering another world entirely.

Maps covered the walls, their carefully inked shores and trading routes speaking of distant adventures. A massive globe dominated one corner, while the opposite wall housed floor-to-ceiling bookcases filled with leather-bound volumes. But it was the chart table that drew her eye—covered in star charts and navigation instruments that made her fingers itch to explore.

"You're shivering," Marcus observed, moving to stoke the fire.

"I'm quite well," Katherine replied automatically, though her wet skirts clung unpleasantly to her legs. She distracted herself by moving closer to examine the charts, recognizing astronomical calculations similar to those she worked on in secret.

Lightning illuminated the room, followed almost immediately

by thunder that rattled the windows. Katherine started, taking an instinctive step backward—directly into Marcus's solid chest.

His hands steadied her shoulders, the touch lasting a heartbeat too long before propriety reasserted itself. "My apologies," he murmured, stepping away. "I was about to point out this particular chart. The star positions are fascinating, though I believe there may be an error in the calculations."

Katherine leaned closer, grateful for the familiar territory of mathematics. "Yes, I see it. The declination is off by several degrees, which would put the vessel significantly off course."

She felt rather than saw Marcus's surprise. "You understand celestial navigation?"

"My late husband encouraged my interest in astronomy," Katherine admitted. "Though I generally confine my calculations to paper rather than practical application."

"A shame," Marcus said softly. "Your mind is wasted on mere social calculations."

The words hung between them, heavy with meaning. Katherine kept her eyes fixed on the chart, though she was acutely aware of his presence just behind her shoulder. The rain drummed against the windows, creating an oddly intimate atmosphere in the fire-lit study.

"Did you encounter many storms at sea?" she asked, desperate to maintain some semblance of proper conversation.

"More than I can count," Marcus replied, his voice dropping lower. "Though none quite as dangerous as this moment."

Katherine's breath caught. She should step away, maintain proper distance, but her feet seemed rooted to the spot. "Mr.

Pembroke mentioned your reputation for steering ships safely through treacherous waters."

"The trick is knowing when to fight the current—" His words brushed her ear, sending a shiver down her spine that had nothing to do with her damp clothing. "—and when to let it carry you where you're meant to go."

The door opened, admitting Mrs. Fletcher with tea and putting a necessary end to the charged moment. Katherine moved away from the chart table on unsteady legs, accepting a cup with grateful hands. The housekeeper's presence restored proper distance between them, but she could still feel the ghost of Marcus's breath on her neck, the phantom pressure of his hands on her shoulders.

Their eyes met over the rim of her teacup, and Katherine saw her own dangerous yearning reflected in his grey gaze. The storm raged outside, but the real tempest, she realized, was just beginning to break within her heart.

The storm's fury had finally begun to subside, the thunder now a distant rumble rather than the violent crashes that had driven Katherine to seek shelter. She set down her empty teacup with hands that trembled slightly, though whether from the lingering chill or something else entirely, she dared not examine too closely.

"I should return home," Katherine said, smoothing her now-dried skirts. "Charlotte will be wondering where I've gone."

"Of course," Marcus moved to the window, studying the breaking clouds. "Though perhaps wait a few more moments to ensure the rain has truly passed."

Mrs. Fletcher had discreetly withdrawn some minutes ago, leaving them alone in the study that seemed to have shrunk in size since Katherine's arrival. The fire crackled in the grate, casting dancing shadows across the maps and charts that had provided such convenient distraction during the storm's height.

Katherine forced herself to walk to the door with measured steps, though her heart beat an erratic rhythm against her ribs. "I've imposed upon your hospitality long enough."

"Katherine."

Her name on his lips stopped her as surely as if he'd grabbed her arm. She turned, finding him much closer than she'd expected, close enough that she could see the flecks of darker grey in his eyes.

"You haven't imposed." His voice had dropped to that dangerous lower register that seemed to bypass her ears entirely and settle somewhere in her chest. "You could never impose."

"We shouldn't—" Katherine began, but the words died in her throat as Marcus closed the remaining distance between them.

His hands found her waist, drawing her against him with a gentleness that somehow made it more devastating than if he'd been rough. Katherine's fingers splayed against his chest, whether to push him away or pull him closer, she wasn't certain.

"Tell me to stop," Marcus murmured, his breath warm against her temple. "Tell me you don't feel this too."

Katherine's response was lost as his mouth found hers. The kiss started softly, almost reverently, but quickly blazed into something far more dangerous. His arms tightened around her as she melted against him, one hand sliding up to cradle the back of her head.

Years of propriety and carefully maintained control shattered like glass. Katherine's fingers curled into the fabric of his coat, bringing them impossibly closer. Marcus groaned against her mouth, deepening the kiss with a passion that stole what little breath remained in her lungs.

This was madness—complete and utter madness. She was a respectable widow, a mother with a daughter to launch into society. She had no business being pressed against an Earl in his study, letting him kiss her as if he would die without the taste of her lips.

Yet she couldn't seem to stop. Every brush of his tongue against hers sent sparks of electricity down her spine. His hands burned through the fabric of her dress, leaving imprints she was certain would be visible to anyone who looked at her. The solid warmth of his chest against hers made her feel simultaneously safer and more dangerous than she'd ever felt in her life.

Marcus pulled back just enough to trail kisses along her jaw, down the column of her throat. "Do you know how long I've wanted to do this?" he whispered against her skin. "How many times I've imagined holding you like this?"

"Marcus," his name came out somewhere between a plea and a prayer. Katherine's head fell back, giving him better access to the sensitive spot below her ear that made her shiver. "We can't—this isn't—"

"Proper?" He lifted his head, meeting her gaze with eyes dark with desire. "No, it isn't proper at all. But it's real, Katherine. This is real."

K atherine's late arrival at Lady Millicent's drawing room caused exactly the ripple of speculation she had dreaded. Though she had taken time to change her rain-dampened clothing and restore her hair to perfect order, she could feel the weight of knowing glances and half-hidden smirks behind painted fans.

"My dear Lady Ashworth," Lady Constance's voice cut through the general murmur of conversation. "We were all quite concerned when your butler said you had been delayed by the storm." Her smile was a masterpiece of false sympathy. "How fortunate that Lord Rutherford's house was so... conveniently situated."

Katherine met the implied accusation with practiced serenity. "Indeed. The Dowager Countess is always most gracious in offering shelter to her acquaintances." The lie slipped easily, though she still tasted Marcus' on her lips.

"Mama!" Charlotte's voice carried clear across the drawing room, pitched just a touch too loud. "Lord Winters absolutely insists that you hear his new composition immediately."

Katherine recognized her daughter's tactical intervention, but the obvious manipulation only drew more attention. Charlotte was practically dragging the bewildered young lord toward the pianoforte, her smile brittle and her eyes feverish with determination to be the center of attention.

"Perhaps another time," Katherine began, but Charlotte had already seated Lord Winters at the instrument.

"No, no, he must play now. Everyone wants to hear it, don't they?" Charlotte's gaze swept the room imperiously, daring anyone to contradict her.

The Dowager Countess of Rutherford chose that moment to make her entrance, her timing suspiciously perfect. "My dear Katherine," she called out, sailing across the room with remarkable speed for a woman of her years. "I was just telling my son how delightful it was to have you take shelter with us during that dreadful storm. Mrs. Fletcher was quite beside herself with joy at having company for her morning chocolate."

Katherine caught the older woman's quick wink, even as she felt Lady Constance's calculating gaze boring into her back. Before she could respond, Lord Winters began to play—a discordant crash of notes that made several listeners wince.

"Charming," Charlotte declared too loudly, though the poor man had barely completed four bars. "Isn't it charming, Mama? So... original."

Katherine watched her daughter's increasingly desperate attempts to command the room's attention, her heart aching. *This was her fault,* she realized. Years of focusing solely on Charlotte had created this hunger for constant validation.

"Perhaps we might step out for a moment," she murmured to Charlotte, reaching for her arm.

"No!" Charlotte jerked away, her voice sharp enough to draw every eye in the room. "I mean, we mustn't interrupt Lord Winters's performance. It would be terribly rude."

The young man in question hit another sour note, his face reddening as he fumbled through the piece.

"I believe," the Dowager Countess announced firmly, "that the rain has quite stopped. Lady Sophia, my dear, would you be so kind as to accompany Miss Ashworth to view the new rose garden? I'm told the blooms are particularly fine after a good soaking."

Lady Sophia rose immediately, her quiet grace a stark contrast to Charlotte's barely contained agitation. "Of course, your grace. Charlotte, you simply must see the new yellow variety. I believe it's the same shade as that lovely gown you admired at Madame Delafield's."

For a moment, Katherine thought Charlotte would refuse. But Lady Sophia's gentle persistence won out, and Charlotte allowed herself to be led from the room, though not without a final glance of reproach at her mother.

The awkward performance at the pianoforte mercifully ended, and conversation gradually resumed. Katherine engaged Lady Millicent in a careful discussion of the upcoming hospital benefit, all while acutely aware of Lady Constance moving through the room like a shark scenting blood in the water.

"You handle her with remarkable patience," the Dowager Countess murmured, taking the seat beside Katherine. "Both of them, in fact."

Katherine didn't pretend to misunderstand. "Charlotte is young," she replied softly. "And Lady Constance... well, she is who she is."

"And you, my dear?" The older woman's shrewd eyes held a mixture of sympathy and challenge. "Who are you, when you're not being Charlotte's mother or society's perfect widow?"

CHAPTER TEN
DREAMS & NIGHTMARES

Katherine found sanctuary in her private study, though even here she could not entirely escape the lingering effects of the morning's events. The scent of rain still hung in the air, and distant thunder growled like her own unsettled thoughts.

Katherine pressed her fingers to her lips, still tingling from Marcus's kiss the night before. The memory of his mouth on hers, firm yet gentle, sent a shiver down her spine. Her breath caught as she recalled how his strong hands had cradled her face, how his body had pressed against hers in the shadowed alcove of his library.

Thank heavens she had found the strength to pull away. One more moment of weakness and she might have followed him upstairs, propriety be damned. The thought made her cheeks flush. She had not been with a man since James died five years ago, and her body's reaction to Marcus's touch had shocked her with its intensity.

Katherine stood and paced the length of her study, trying to dispel the heat coursing through her veins. But each step only brought fresh memories: the rough silk of his cravat beneath her fingers, the solid warmth of his chest, the way his breath had hitched when she'd gasped against his mouth.

"This is madness," she whispered to the empty room, but her traitorous mind conjured images of Marcus's hands sliding lower, of his lips trailing down her neck, of their bodies entwined without the barrier of clothing between them.

She sank into her chair, pressing her cool palms to her burning cheeks. James had been a kind man, a gentle lover, but in fifteen years of marriage, he had never made her feel like this—wild and wanton and desperately alive. He had never sparked this aching need that made her forget she was a respectable widow and mother.

Marcus was different. Even now, alone in her study, the mere thought of him made her pulse race. She imagined his hands, strong and sure from years at sea, exploring her body with the same careful attention he gave to charting stars. His mouth, so clever in conversation, finding new ways to make her gasp and sigh.

Katherine squeezed her eyes shut, but that only made the images more vivid. Marcus removing her pins one by one until her hair tumbled down her back. His fingers tracing the curve of her spine, the swell of her breast. His voice, deep and rough with desire, whispering her name against her skin.

"Get hold of yourself," she muttered, forcing her eyes open. But her body hummed with awareness, with a need she had never known existed before Marcus crashed into her carefully ordered world.

She could still feel the phantom press of his lips, still taste tea on his tongue, still hear the low groan that had rumbled through his chest when she'd threaded her fingers through his hair.

The clock chimed the quarter hour, making her jump. Katherine pressed a hand to her racing heart, trying to slow its frantic rhythm. She was a grown woman, not some green girl experiencing her first flutterings of desire. *But oh, how she wanted him.* The wanting frightened her with its intensity, with how quickly it had overcome her usual sensible nature.

She rose again, needing to move, to do something to distract herself from these overwhelming sensations. But every step reminded her of how it felt to be held in Marcus's strong embrace, how perfectly they fit together, how right it had felt despite all the reasons it was wrong.

She willed herself to concentrate and was halfway through the estate ledgers when Mrs. Davis appeared at the door, her usually composed face pinched with concern. "Begging your pardon, my lady, but Miss Charlotte..."

Katherine set down her pen with practiced calm, though her heart quickened. "Yes?"

"She's in quite a state, my lady. Found her attempting to slip out the garden gate not ten minutes ago. When I questioned her, she flew into such a temper—" The housekeeper wrung her hands. "She's locked herself in the late viscount's study."

Of course she had. Charlotte had always retreated there when upset as a child, curling up in her father's old chair as if she could conjure his comfort through proximity alone. Katherine rose, smoothing her skirts with hands that trembled only slightly.

"I'll speak with her."

She found Charlotte exactly where she expected—ensconced in James's leather chair, though she looked less like a grieving daughter seeking solace and more like a general plotting battle strategy. Papers were strewn across the normally immaculate desk, and Katherine recognized the elaborate loops of Charlotte's correspondence.

"I suppose you've come to lecture me about my behavior at Lady Millicent's," Charlotte said without looking up.

"Actually, I came to ask why you felt the need to slip out through the garden gate rather than use the front door." Katherine kept her voice gentle, though her stomach clenched at the implications.

Charlotte's quill scratched against paper with unnecessary force. "Perhaps I simply wanted some air without an audience of servants reporting my every movement."

"To whom were you writing?"

"That's private."

"Nothing is private when your reputation is at stake." Katherine moved closer, catching a glimpse of multiple sheets in the same masculine hand before Charlotte could gather them up. "Who is he?"

"Why should you care?" Charlotte's chin lifted in defiance. "You're too busy with your own romantic intrigues to concern yourself with mine."

The accusation landed like a physical blow. "Charlotte—"

"Don't deny it. I've heard the whispers. Seen you two look at one another at Lady Millicent's, as if no one else existed." Charlotte's voice cracked. "You used to look at *me* that way."

Before Katherine could respond, a sharp knock at the door heralded Marcus's unexpected arrival. He stood framed in the doorway, his expression shifting rapidly from determination to awareness of the charged atmosphere he'd interrupted.

"My apologies," he said formally. "Your butler indicated you were reviewing business matters—"

"How convenient that business requires such frequent visits," Charlotte cut in, her tone arctic. "Tell me, Lord Rutherford, do all your business associates receive such personal attention, or only the beautiful widowed ones?"

"Charlotte!" Katherine's shock barely registered before Charlotte had gathered her letters and swept past them both, leaving behind the lingering echo of her bitter words and the heavy scent of James's favorite leather chair.

The silence stretched taut between them until Marcus spoke quietly. "I should not have come unannounced."

"No," Katherine agreed, though her heart protested. "You shouldn't have."

He took a step toward her, then seemed to think better of it. "Katherine—"

"Please," she held up a hand, unable to bear whatever he might say when her daughter's pain was still so raw in the air. "Whatever business brought you here must wait for a more appropriate time."

"The business was merely an excuse," he admitted. "After this morning, I needed to see you, to explain—"

"There is nothing to explain," Katherine forced steel into her voice. "This morning was an unfortunate circumstance brought about by weather. Nothing more."

His grey eyes darkened like the storm-laden sky. "We both know that's not true."

"What I know," Katherine said carefully, "is that my daughter believes I have betrayed her. And perhaps she's right."

She turned away, ostensibly to straighten the papers Charlotte had scattered, but truly to hide the treacherous moisture gathering in her eyes. She heard Marcus's sharp intake of breath, as if he would argue further, but the quiet click of the door told her he had gone.

Only then did she allow herself to sink into James's chair, the leather still warm from Charlotte's presence, and press her fingers to her temples. The thunder had moved further away, but the storm in her heart showed no signs of abating.

K atherine found no peace that evening, even in the familiar routines of dinner preparation. The delicate chime of silver against porcelain seemed to mock her attempts at normalcy as Charlotte's chair remained conspicuously empty, her absence a wordless accusation.

"Miss Charlotte is taking a tray in her room," Mrs. Davis announced, though Katherine hadn't asked. "Claims a headache, though if you'll pardon my saying so, my lady, sulking seems a more accurate diagnosis."

Katherine managed a wan smile. "Thank you, Mrs. Davis. I'll look in on her later."

The words had barely left her lips when Thompson appeared in the doorway, his usually impeccable composure slightly ruffled. "Mr. Pembroke to see you, my lady. He insists the matter cannot wait until morning."

Katherine's fingers tightened on her napkin. Of all the unwelcome interruptions this evening might have produced, Thomas Pembroke ranked among the worst. Yet there was something in Thompson's manner that suggested more than mere social inconvenience.

"Show him to the morning room," she said, rising. "And have tea brought in."

She found Marcus's cousin pacing before the fireplace, his elegant evening clothes suggesting he'd abandoned some social engagement to make this call. His expression, when he turned to face her, held none of his usual smooth charm.

"Lady Ashworth," he executed a bow that managed to be both precise and somehow urgent. "I must beg your forgiveness for this unconventional visit, but I felt you should be warned."

"Warned?" Katherine gestured for him to take a seat, but he remained standing, his agitation palpable.

"About Marcus," Pembroke ran a hand through his carefully styled hair. "His... attachment to you has become obvious to those who know him well. And while I'm sure your influence is entirely innocent, you should know that his position is more precarious than it appears."

Katherine felt ice form in her stomach. "I'm afraid I don't take your meaning, sir."

"The shipping company faces certain... difficulties. Difficulties that require Marcus's complete attention and perhaps some advantageous connections through marriage." His eyes fixed on her face. "Lady Constance's family, for instance, has extensive holdings in the Indies."

"I see," Katherine's voice remained steady through years of practice. "And you felt this information couldn't wait until a more appropriate hour?"

"Not when I observed him leaving your house this afternoon." Pembroke's expression shifted to something approaching sympathy. "Think of your daughter, my lady. How would Charlotte's prospects be affected if her mother became entangled in a business scandal?"

As if summoned by her name, Charlotte's voice drifted down from the upper hall, followed by the sound of a door opening. Pembroke's eyes darted to the ceiling, then back to Katherine with unmistakable meaning.

"I appreciate your... concern," Katherine said, rising to signal the end of the interview. "Though I confess I'm puzzled why you chose to bring this warning to me rather than discuss these business matters with your cousin directly."

"Marcus can be stubborn when his emotions are engaged." Pembroke moved toward the door, then paused. "He's not the man you imagine him to be, Lady Ashworth. The years in China changed him in ways that would shock polite society. Ways that could destroy everything you've built for Charlotte."

He left her standing in the middle of her morning room, the tea service arriving moments too late to serve its purpose. Katherine sank onto the settee, her mind racing between Pembroke's warnings, Charlotte's pain, and the memory of Marcus's face when she'd dismissed him that afternoon.

The rational part of her knew Pembroke's visit had been carefully calculated to achieve maximum effect. Yet she couldn't quite dismiss the kernel of truth buried within his implications. Everything she'd built, everything she'd sacrificed to secure Charlotte's future, balanced on the knife's edge of society's approval.

One mistake, one scandal, and it would all crumble like a house of cards in a summer storm.

The night wrapped Ashworth House in darkness broken only by occasional flashes of distant lightning. Katherine stood at her bedroom window, watching the remnants of the storm paint silver edges on the clouds scudding past. Sleep seemed an impossible prospect with her thoughts churning like the weather-troubled sky.

A soft knock interrupted her vigil. "Mama?" Charlotte's voice carried none of its earlier venom. "Are you awake?"

Katherine opened the door to find her daughter in her night rail, looking young and vulnerable in a way that squeezed her heart. "Another nightmare?"

Charlotte nodded, and for a moment she was six years old again, seeking comfort after her father's death. "I heard the thunder and..." She twisted her fingers in her dressing gown. "May I stay with you? Just for a little while?"

They settled on Katherine's bed as they had so many times before, Charlotte's head resting against her shoulder. The familiar scent of lavender water in her daughter's hair brought a fresh wave of maternal tenderness.

"I'm sorry," Charlotte whispered into the darkness. "About what I said earlier. I didn't mean—"

"Hush," Katherine stroked her daughter's hair. "I know you didn't."

Thunder rolled again, closer now, and Charlotte tensed. "Do you remember how Papa used to tell me the thunder was just angels rearranging furniture in heaven?"

"And you asked if they ever managed to get it right, or if we'd have to listen to them moving things forever." The shared memory brought a bittersweet smile to Katherine's lips.

A particularly bright flash of lightning illuminated the room, followed almost immediately by a tremendous crash that rattled the windows. Charlotte burrowed closer.

AFTERNOON TEA

K atherine stepped into the garden observatory, where raindrops created a gentle symphony against the glass walls. Spring flowers perfumed the air, their fragrance mingling with the steam rising from freshly brewed tea. She adjusted a spray of pale pink roses, ensuring the setting met her exacting standards for the afternoon's gathering.

The Dowager Countess swept in first, her silver-streaked hair gleaming beneath an elaborate turban. "My dear Katherine, how clever of you to choose this enchanting space. Though I dare say Marcus would have appreciated the astronomical implications."

Katherine's heart stuttered at the mention of his name, but she maintained her composure. "Indeed, though I believe the weather would have rendered stargazing quite impossible today."

The Carmichaels arrived next, bringing their characteristic exuberance. Mrs. Carmichael immediately began extolling the virtues of the glass paneling, while her husband examined the construction with keen interest.

Lord Ridlington entered supporting his grandmother's arm, his hazel eyes warm as he assisted her to a comfortable chair. The elderly lady patted his hand with obvious affection before turning to greet Katherine.

Charlotte burst into the room in a swirl of pale blue muslin, her brown curls bouncing with each animated step. "Lady Ridlington, how wonderful you could join us! And Lord Ridlington, you simply must tell me about your latest architectural project."

Katherine watched as her daughter drew Lord Ridlington into conversation, noting how his reserved manner softened in response to Charlotte's enthusiasm. Their heads bent together as he described something with careful gestures, Charlotte's laugh ringing out like silver bells.

"Young Henry has grown into quite the gentleman," the Dowager observed, accepting a cup of tea. "His dedication to his grandmother speaks well of his character."

"Indeed," Mrs. Carmichael chimed in, "though one might wish he attended more social functions. Still, such devotion to family cannot be faulted."

The rain intensified, drumming against the glass roof and creating an intimate atmosphere that encouraged confidence. Conversation flowed easily among the guests, punctuated by gentle laughter and the clink of fine china.

"I must say," the Dowager proclaimed, raising her cup, "that we are witnessing the emergence of a true diamond of the first water. To Miss Charlotte Ashworth, may your Season continue to sparkle as brightly as you do."

Charlotte's cheeks flushed prettily as she accepted the toast, though Katherine detected a flutter of uncertainty beneath her daughter's practiced smile. Lord Ridlington's quiet words of encouragement seemed to steady her, and Katherine felt the familiar tangle of maternal pride and concern twist in her chest.

A sudden gust of wind drove the rain harder against the glass, creating rivulets that cast dancing shadows across the gathering. "How atmospheric," Mrs. Carmichael declared with delight. "Though I dare say some might find a reason to be fashionably late in such weather."

Katherine determinedly ignored the pointed reference to Marcus's absence, busying herself instead with directing the footman to replenish the tea service. She couldn't help but notice how Lord Ridlington had drawn Charlotte into a discussion about music, his genuine interest evident in his attentive expression.

The peaceful moment shattered when the footman stumbled, nearly upending the tea tray. Quick reflexes saved the china, but not before eliciting a collective gasp from the gathering.

"Well," the Dowager drawled, "I see we're to be treated to some impromptu entertainment. Though I must say, I prefer my tea in cups rather than on carpets."

The tension dissolved into laughter, and Katherine found herself grateful for the Dowager's quick wit. She watched as Charlotte touched Lord Ridlington's arm while sharing in the merriment, her daughter's natural vivacity drawing others into her orbit.

Katherine noticed Albert Carmichael's approach before Charlotte did. He moved with the practiced grace of a young man who knew precisely how handsome he appeared, his light brown hair artfully tousled despite the dampness in the air.

"Miss Ashworth," Albert's voice carried across the observatory with perfect pitch. "I happened upon the most fascinating article about the new theater production. I recalled your interest in the arts."

Charlotte barely glanced up from her conversation with Lord Ridlington. "How thoughtful, Mr. Carmichael. Though Lord Ridlington was just explaining the most intriguing details about Roman architecture."

Albert's smile didn't falter. "Ah, but this production features that actress you admired so thoroughly at Lady Winchester's last week. The one playing Juliet?" He paused deliberately. "I hear she's to give private performances for select members of society."

Charlotte's head snapped up, her attention finally caught. "Private performances? But surely those are impossible to attend?"

"Not impossible at all," Albert's blue eyes sparkled with mischief. "In fact, I have it on good authority that arrangements could be made for the right patron."

Lord Ridlington shifted in his seat, a slight furrow appearing between his brows. "Miss Ashworth, regarding the architectural elements we were discussing—"

"Oh!" Charlotte rose, her whole bearing transformed by sudden animation. "Mr. Carmichael, you must tell me more. Shall we examine mother's new rose varieties? The rain has nearly stopped."

Katherine watched as Albert offered his arm with a flourish, leading Charlotte toward the garden door. She caught the flash of disappointment across Lord Ridlington's features before he schooled them back to polite neutrality.

Katherine watched the garden door close behind Charlotte and Albert with growing unease. The rain had picked up again, fat drops now pelting against the glass panes with increasing urgency. Her fingers tightened around her teacup as she fought the instinct to rush after them.

"They'll be soaked through," she murmured, half-rising from her seat. The thought of Charlotte catching a chill—or worse, ruining her new muslin gown—warred with her awareness of how a mother's interference might be perceived.

The Dowager's hand settled on her wrist, keeping her in place. She leaned close, her voice pitched for Katherine's ears alone. "Give her a moment dear, allow the seeds to plant themselves."

Katherine's brow furrowed. "I'm not certain I take your meaning."

"Don't you?" The Dowager's knowing look spoke volumes. "Young people must sometimes learn through their own mistakes. Though I dare say getting caught in the rain with Mr. Carmichael might prove most illuminating for all parties concerned."

Understanding dawned as Katherine glanced at Lord Ridlington, who had taken up conversation with Mrs. Carmichael but whose attention clearly strayed to the garden door every few moments. The slight tension in his jaw betrayed his own carefully masked concern.

"I suppose you're right," Katherine conceded, though she couldn't quite suppress a small sigh. "Still, one hopes the lesson won't come at too dear a price."

"My dear, some prices must be paid for wisdom." The Dowager settled back in her chair with the air of one who had orchestrated a particularly clever move in a game of chess. "Though I must say, your observatory provides an excellent vantage point for watching such lessons unfold."

Indeed, through the rain-streaked glass, Katherine could make out the forms of Charlotte and Albert as they ducked beneath the inadequate shelter of a rose arbor. Charlotte's animated gestures suggested she was fully engaged in whatever tale Albert spun, while Lord Ridlington's presence in the observatory seemed to have been entirely forgotten.

"I don't recall Mr. Carmichael showing such interest in the theater before today," Katherine observed quietly.

The Dowager's lips quirked. "How fascinating that his cultural pursuits should align so perfectly with your daughter's interests. One might almost suspect careful study of her preferences."

Mrs. Carmichael's voice carried across the room, sharp with maternal pride. "Albert has always been passionate about the arts. Why, just the other day he was expounding upon the merits of various playhouses."

Katherine caught the slight roll of Lord Ridlington's eyes before he masked it with a polite cough. His grandmother patted his arm sympathetically, her own expression suggesting she shared his skepticism regarding Albert's newfound theatrical expertise.

The rain drummed harder against the glass, and Charlotte's laugh carried faintly through the downpour. Katherine watched as Albert drew closer to her daughter, presumably to better shelter her from the weather. Lord Ridlington's posture stiffened almost imperceptibly.

"Perhaps someone should offer them an umbrella," he suggested, his tone carefully neutral.

"Oh, I'm certain they'll come in when they're ready," the Dowager interjected before Katherine could respond. "Young people can be so resistant to interference in their private conversations."

Katherine noticed how Lord Ridlington's fingers tightened briefly around his teacup at the word 'private.' She found herself wondering if the Dowager's orchestration extended beyond this afternoon's gathering.

"More tea, Lord Ridlington?" she offered, partly to distract herself from the scene in the garden.

"Thank you, Lady Katherine." His smile carried a hint of gratitude for the momentary reprieve from watching Charlotte's tête-à-tête with Albert.

As Katherine poured, she caught the Dowager's approving nod. Outside, Charlotte and Albert remained engrossed in conversation, seemingly oblivious to both the weather and their audience. The rain continued its steady percussion against the glass, creating a strange intimacy in the observatory despite—or perhaps because of—the rising tension among its occupants.

"I dare say this weather will persist through the evening," Mrs. Carmichael observed. "Albert mentioned something about tickets to the theater tonight. Perhaps we should send a carriage for Miss Ashworth, should she wish to attend?"

Before Katherine could formulate a diplomatic response, Lord Ridlington spoke up. "I believe my grandmother had expressed interest in this evening's performance as well. Might I offer our carriage for the ladies?"

I n the garden, sheltered by a generous umbrella Albert had produced from seemingly nowhere, Charlotte found herself drawn into his enthusiastic description of the theater's inner workings. He painted a picture of glamour and intrigue that made her previous conversation about Roman columns seem terribly dull in comparison.

"You should see how the mechanism works," Albert demonstrated with his free hand, nearly dropping the umbrella. "Oh! Careful there," he caught Charlotte as she stumbled slightly on the wet path, his hand lingering perhaps a moment longer than strictly necessary on her arm.

Charlotte felt heat rise to her cheeks. "You seem to know an awful lot about the theater, Mr. Carmichael."

"Albert, please. At least when we're away from the watchful eyes of society." His smile turned softer, more intimate. "I find myself wanting to share all sorts of things with you, Miss Ashworth. You have a way of making even the most mundane topics fascinating."

"Charlotte," she offered in return, her voice barely above a whisper. "When we're away from watchful eyes, of course."

They paused beneath a dripping arbor, the roses nodding heavy heads above them. Albert's expression grew serious, surprising

Charlotte with its sudden gravity. "You know, everyone sees you as this bright, glittering star of the Season. And you are, of course you are. But I suspect there's so much more to you than that."

Charlotte found herself staring into his bright blue eyes, caught off guard by this glimpse of depth beneath his usual charming facade. "I... what makes you say that?"

"The way you light up when discussing real passions, like theater. The clever things you say when you forget to be proper. The kindness I've seen you show to those less fortunate." Albert's voice had dropped lower, more sincere than she'd ever heard it. "I notice these things about you, Charlotte."

She felt her breath catch, suddenly aware of how close they stood beneath the umbrella's shelter. Raindrops fell around them in a gentle curtain, creating an intimate world of their own.

"Most people don't look past the surface," Charlotte admitted, surprising herself with her honesty. "It's easier to be what they expect."

"Then most people are fools," Albert said simply, reaching out to catch a raindrop that had fallen on her cheek. "I find myself wanting to know every layer of your character, even the ones you hide from society."

Charlotte's heart fluttered as she studied Albert's face, seeing him truly for the first time. The rain had darkened his light brown hair to honey, and droplets clung to his long eyelashes. *How had she never noticed the perfect curve of his jaw before? Or the way his blue eyes sparkled with barely contained mischief?*

He wasn't just the wealthy tradesman's son anymore—he was fascinating. The way he spoke about the theater revealed depths she hadn't expected, and his genuine interest in her thoughts made her feel seen in a way Lord Ridlington's architectural discussions never had.

"You're staring," Albert murmured, his lips curving into a knowing smile that sent warmth spreading through her chest.

"I'm observing," Charlotte corrected, proud that her voice remained steady despite the trembling in her hands. "Since you seem so keen on noticing things about me, it seems only fair I return the favor."

Albert shifted closer, adjusting the umbrella. The movement brought his arm within inches of hers, and Charlotte's breath caught at the proximity. Every small gesture—the flex of his fingers on the umbrella handle, the slight tilt of his head as he regarded her—drew her attention like a moth to flame.

"And what do you observe, Miss Charlotte?" The playful formality in his tone made her name sound like a caress.

She became acutely aware of how the damp air made her skin hypersensitive. The brush of her muslin gown against her arms felt electric, and she could swear she felt the heat radiating from Albert's body despite the inches between them.

"I observe that you're far more interesting than Roman columns," Charlotte said, earning a rich laugh that made her stomach flip pleasantly.

"High praise indeed, considering how attentively you were listening to Lord Ridlington's discourse on architecture." His eyes crinkled at the corners when he smiled—another detail she'd somehow missed before.

Charlotte barely remembered her earlier conversation with Lord Ridlington. It seemed impossibly dull compared to the crackling energy between her and Albert now. Her gaze dropped to his lips as he spoke, watching how they shaped each word with devastating precision.

"Perhaps I simply needed the right subject to capture my attention," she said softly.

Albert's smile faded slightly, replaced by something more intense. His eyes flickered to her mouth, and Charlotte felt her lips part instinctively. The rain seemed to fall harder around their little shelter, but she barely noticed, too consumed by the way Albert swayed almost imperceptibly closer.

"And have you found it?" he asked, his voice rough around the edges. "The right subject?"

Charlotte's pulse thundered in her ears. The space between them had shrunk to nearly nothing, and she found herself tilting her face up toward his, drawn by a force as inevitable as gravity. "I believe I might have."

Albert's free hand rose to hover near her cheek, not quite touching but close enough that she could feel the promise of contact. His eyes held hers, dark with an emotion that made her knees weak. Time seemed to slow, measured only by the steady drumming of rain against the umbrella and the rapid beating of her heart.

Their breaths mingled in the humid air as Charlotte's world narrowed to the microscopic distance between their lips. She could count every shade of blue in his eyes at this distance, could see the slight tremor in his hand as it remained suspended near her face.

The moment stretched like spun sugar, sweet and fragile. Charlotte felt herself sway forward, her eyes beginning to flutter closed—

A crack of thunder shattered the silence, making them both jump. The spell broke, and Albert straightened, though his eyes remained fixed on her face with an intensity that made her shiver despite the warm air.

"We should return to the observatory," he said, his voice still carrying that delicious roughness. "Before we're missed."

Charlotte nodded, not trusting herself to speak. As they walked back, sharing the umbrella and carefully not touching, she was exquisitely aware of every movement he made, every breath he took. Lord Ridlington and his architectural expertise had faded completely from her mind, replaced entirely by the overwhelming presence of Albert Carmichael and the lingering question of what might have happened if the thunder hadn't interrupted them.

AN UNEXPECTED TURN

Katherine sat at her writing desk in the Morning Room, the steady patter of rain against the windows creating a soothing backdrop as she sorted through the morning's correspondence. Pale sunlight filtered through the gauzy curtains, catching on the delicate bone china tea service and highlighting the fresh spring blooms arranged in crystal vases. A letter from her sister-in-law regarding the upcoming garden party at their country estate lay half-read before her.

Charlotte's restless pacing drew Katherine's attention from her task. Her daughter's silk morning dress rustled with each turn, her fingers twisting together in an uncharacteristic display of nerves.

"Mama, I do not see the point in waiting! What is a girl to do while a suitable gentleman dithers?" Charlotte's voice carried an edge of urgency that made Katherine look up sharply from her letters.

Katherine set down her pen, studying her daughter's flushed

cheeks. "Charlotte, you must remember that haste can often lead to errors. A proper courtship requires patience."

Charlotte let out an exasperated sigh and dropped onto the settee, her skirts billowing around her. "But Mama, Lady Somerset's daughter already has three callers, and she made her debut after me." She picked at an invisible thread on her sleeve. "Even that dreadful Miss Fairfax has gentleman leaving cards."

Katherine pressed her lips together, suppressing the urge to remind her daughter about proper deportment. "My dear, a lady does not count her callers against others. Besides, you had Lord Ridlington's undivided attention at the observatory gathering."

"Lord Ridlington?" Charlotte's nose wrinkled. "He's perfectly pleasant, but surely you cannot expect me to settle for merely pleasant."

"I expect you to give each gentleman fair consideration." Katherine's tone carried a note of warning. "The Season has only begun. There will be countless opportunities to make advantageous connections."

Charlotte sprang up from her seat and moved to the window, pressing her forehead against the cool glass. "But what if the best opportunities have already passed? What if—" She broke off, her shoulders tensing. "What if I've already missed my chance with... certain gentlemen?"

Katherine's hand stilled over her letters. "There are three more major balls this month alone, not to mention Lady Hutchinson's musical evening and the Pembroke family's garden party."

"The Pembrokes?" Charlotte turned, her eyes bright with sudden interest. "Will Thomas Pembroke be in attendance?"

"Charlotte," Katherine's voice hardened. "Lord Rutherford's attendance is hardly relevant to your prospects."

"But everyone says he's the most eligible—"

"Everyone says a great many things, most of which are better left unsaid." Katherine rose from her desk, crossing to where her daughter stood. "You would do well to focus on gentlemen closer to your own age and circumstances."

Charlotte's lower lip protruded. "I don't see why I should limit myself. After all, you've caught the Earl's attention often enough."

The accusation hung in the air between them. Katherine drew in a careful breath. "That is neither appropriate nor accurate. Now, shall we discuss your attendance at these upcoming events, or would you prefer to continue making improper observations?"

"Fine," Charlotte moved away from the window, her fingers trailing along the wallpaper. "But I want new gowns. I cannot be expected to make an impression in anything I've already worn."

"You have plenty of perfectly suitable—"

"Mama, please," Charlotte's voice took on the wheedling tone that had worked so well in her childhood. "Just think how well I could show at Lady Hutchinson's if I had that new French silk Madame Delacore just received. The pale blue would set off my eyes beautifully."

Katherine returned to her desk, picking up her pen. "We shall see. First, you must demonstrate that you understand the proper way to conduct yourself in society."

"I always conduct myself properly!" Charlotte protested.

"Need I remind you of your behavior at the musical evening?"

Charlotte's cheeks flushed. "That was different. I was merely trying to—"

"To draw attention to yourself in a most unbecoming manner." Katherine dipped her pen in ink. "If you wish to be taken seriously as a prospective bride, you must first show that you understand the responsibilities that come with such a position."

"But Mama—"

"No, Charlotte. I will hear no more on the subject today. We have calls to make this afternoon, and I expect you to display the grace and charm I know you possess."

Charlotte stormed up the stairs to her bedchamber, each step punctuating her frustration. The steady drumming of rain against the windows matched the thundering of her heart as she flung herself onto the window seat, pressing her forehead against the cool glass.

Beyond the rain-streaked pane, London stretched out in shades of grey, the usually bustling streets emptied by the weather. She felt as caged as the little finches Mrs. Winters kept in her drawing room, forever batting their wings against gilded bars.

"It isn't fair," she whispered to her reflection. The pale face that stared back bore little resemblance to the vivacious beauty everyone praised. Instead, she saw uncertainty in her eyes, a trembling in her lower lip that betrayed her fears.

Lord Ridlington had smiled at her so warmly at the observatory gathering. And Mr. Carmichael's eyes had sparkled with such mischief during their last dance. *Why should she wait for them to make their intentions known? What if they thought her indifferent? What if they turned their attentions elsewhere while she sat here, bound by propriety?*

Charlotte pushed away from the window, energy coursing through her veins. Her writing desk beckoned from the corner, its rosewood surface gleaming in the grey light. She could pen two notes—nothing too forward, of course. Just friendly correspondence to remind them of her existence.

Her fingers trembled as she withdrew her finest writing paper from the drawer. The cream-colored sheets seemed to glow against the dark wood. She selected her best pen, the one Papa had given her for her sixteenth birthday, its mother-of-pearl handle cool against her palm.

To Lord Ridlington first, she decided. His quiet nature meant he might need more encouragement. She would mention how much she had enjoyed their discussion of astronomy. Perhaps add something about hoping to further their acquaintance at Lady Hutchinson's musical evening.

And then to Mr. Carmichael—dear Albert, with his ready laugh and dancing eyes. She could reference their shared appreciation for Byron's poetry, maybe even quote a particularly romantic verse...

The door creaked open behind her. Charlotte's hand jerked, sending an ink blot sprawling across the pristine paper.

"Charlotte?" Katherine stood in the doorway, one eyebrow raised at the sight of her daughter hunched over the writing desk. "What are you doing?"

Heat flooded Charlotte's cheeks. "I was just... practicing my penmanship."

Katherine glided into the room, her sharp eyes taking in the fresh paper, the uncapped ink, the guilty flush on her daughter's face. "Practicing your penmanship? Or perhaps composing letters that ought not be written?"

"I don't see why I shouldn't write to them," Charlotte burst out, dropping all pretense. "How else will they know I welcome their attention?"

"My dear girl," Katherine's voice softened as she placed a gentle hand on Charlotte's shoulder. "They will know by your manner in company, by your smile when they approach, by the dances you accept. But a lady must never appear eager."

"But what if they mistake my reserve for indifference?" Charlotte twisted in her chair to face her mother. "What if they turn to other ladies who are more... forthcoming with their feelings?"

"Then they are not gentlemen worthy of your regard." Katherine's fingers squeezed lightly. "A man of true quality will understand the delicate dance of courtship. He will respect the proper forms and appreciate a lady who does the same."

"But Mama—"

"No, Charlotte," Katherine's tone brooked no argument. "You must trust that if their interest is genuine, they will make it known in their own time. Any gentleman worth having will pursue you properly, not wait for you to chase after him."

The last words stung, and Charlotte felt fresh color flood her face. "I wasn't going to chase after them! I only meant to..."

"To push fate along?" Katherine's smile held a knowing edge. "Patience, my dear, is often the hardest lesson for a young lady to learn. But it is also the most essential."

. . .

Katherine stood at her bedroom window, watching raindrops trace lazy patterns down the glass. The grey morning perfectly matched her melancholy mood. Her fingers absently traced the delicate lace at her throat, remembering the brush of Marcus's hand there during their last encounter at the British Museum.

How many days had passed since she'd seen him? Seven? Eight? The days blurred together in a haze of social obligations and maternal duties. Yet every gathering felt hollow without his steady presence, his keen observations, the way his eyes would find hers across a crowded room.

She pressed her forehead against the cool windowpane. "This is madness," she whispered to her reflection. *At eight-and-thirty, she was far too old for such girlish pining. What would society say if they knew the widow Ashworth spent her mornings dreaming of stolen kisses in museum corridors?*

That kiss. Her breath caught at the memory. The way he'd drawn her behind closed doors, his fingers gentle on her wrist. The perfect pressure of his lips against hers, tender yet demanding. The warmth of his body pressed...

"My lady?" Mrs. Davis's voice shattered the reverie. "Will you be taking breakfast in your room this morning?"

Katherine straightened, smoothing her expression into careful neutrality. "No, thank you. I'll join Charlotte in the morning room."

Once alone again, she moved to her vanity, studying her reflection with critical eyes. The years had been kind, yes, but she was no debutante. Marcus could have his pick of young, fresh beauties. *Why would he waste his time with a widow whose primary occupation was managing her headstrong daughter?*

Yet she couldn't forget the intensity in his grey eyes when he spoke of navigation and the stars. The way his hand had lingered on hers as they examined ancient astronomical charts. The depth of understanding that passed between them without words.

"Where are you?" she murmured, touching her lips. *Was he avoiding her? Had she imagined the connection between them?* Perhaps he'd already moved on to more suitable prospects.

The thought sent an acute pain through her chest. Love. The word she'd been avoiding rose unbidden in her mind. This wasn't mere attraction or the excitement of forbidden flirtation. Somewhere between scholarly discussions and shared glances, she'd fallen irrevocably in love with Marcus Pembroke, the Earl Rutherford.

Katherine sank onto her bed, pressing her hands against her burning cheeks. The impropriety of it all! A respectable widow pursuing a match with an eligible Earl? The ton would have a field day with such a scandal. She could already hear Lady Jersey's cutting remarks, and see Lady Constance's triumphant smirk.

"Pull yourself together," she commanded her reflection. She was Charlotte's mother first and foremost. Her duty lay in securing her daughter's future, not chasing romantic fantasies like some lovesick girl.

But oh, how she ached to see him again. To feel the brush of his fingers against her arm, to lose herself in conversation about distant lands and ancient wisdom. To experience once more that perfect moment when his lips had claimed hers, making her feel more alive than she had in years.

The morning bell rang, signaling it was time to face another day of propriety and pretense. Katherine rose, straightening her spine and arranging her features into their usual serene mask. She would endure the endless round of morning calls and afternoon teas. She would guide Charlotte through the intricacies of her first Season.

And she would absolutely not think about Marcus Pembroke's kisses.

But as she reached for her door handle, her traitorous heart whispered that she was lying to herself. Every room she entered would be searched for his tall figure. Every conversation would be half-attended, her ears straining for the sound of his distinctive voice. Every moment would be colored by his absence, like a painting missing its most vital hue.

CHAPTER THIRTEEN
KATHERINE

K atherine stood before her own mirror, smoothing the fabric of her morning dress - a becoming shade of deep blue that brought out the green in her eyes. She had chosen it with particular care, though she refused to acknowledge exactly why the selection had occupied so much of her attention this morning.

"The papers you requested, my lady," her maid Martha said, placing a neat stack of correspondence on the side table. "And the cook wishes to know if you'll be dining at home this evening before the assembly."

Katherine was about to respond when the distinct sound of the doorbell echoed through the house. She paused, her hand hovering over the letters, as footsteps hurried up the stairs.

A moment later, a knock came at her door.

"Enter," Katherine called, turning from the mirror.

Martha appeared, slightly breathless. "My lady, the Earl of Rutherford has called."

Katherine's heart performed an entirely inappropriate flutter. She pressed her hands against her skirts, grateful that her complexion didn't easily show a blush. "Did he state his purpose?"

"He mentioned something about discussing the astronomical texts he sent over, my lady. He's waiting in the morning room."

Katherine glanced at the ornate clock on her mantel. It was barely eleven - rather early for social calls, though not inappropriately so. Still, his timing suggested a deliberate choice to arrive before the usual visiting hours when the house would be full of other callers.

"Very well. Please inform his lordship I shall be down directly." Katherine turned back to her mirror, examining her appearance with newfound criticism. "And Martha, perhaps the sapphire earbobs rather than the pearls."

As Martha hurried to make the exchange, Katherine heard Charlotte's voice drift through the walls, humming a romantic air from the latest opera. The sound gave her pause. She hadn't told Charlotte about Marcus's letter, nor her response. While there was nothing improper about discussing shared intellectual interests, Katherine couldn't quite dismiss the flutter of guilt that accompanied her anticipation.

"Shall I inform Miss Charlotte of the Earl's arrival?" Martha asked, helping Katherine with the earrings.

"No need to disturb her while she's with Ellen. I'm sure she'll join us when she's ready." Katherine smoothed her hair one final time. It was the proper response - Charlotte would indeed come down when she finished her toilette - but Katherine couldn't deny the small thrill at the prospect of a few moments alone with Marcus.

The morning room would be perfectly proper, flooded with sunshine and visible from the street. No one could object to two people discussing astronomical calculations in such a setting. And if her pulse quickened at the thought of seeing him, well, that was hardly something anyone else needed to know.

"That will be all, Martha. Please tell his lordship I'll be down momentarily." Katherine gathered her composure along with her fan and gloves. She could hear Charlotte's voice rising in volume as she practiced her scales - clearly in no hurry to conclude her morning routine.

Katherine paused at her bedroom door, checking her reflection one final time in the glass. The sapphires caught the light, adding a becoming sparkle to her appearance. She touched one gently, remembering how Marcus had commented on the color blue at their last meeting, comparing it to the depth of tropical seas he'd sailed.

Charlotte's clear soprano floated down the hallway once more, this time accompanied by the sound of her laughter. The juxtaposition of her daughter's carefree happiness and her own complex emotions regarding Marcus struck Katherine with sudden force. She straightened her shoulders, reminding herself that she was a respectable widow and mother, not some green girl experiencing her first flutter of attraction.

Yet as she moved toward the stairs, Katherine couldn't quite suppress the warmth that spread through her chest at the thought of Marcus waiting below. Their correspondence about the astronomical texts had revealed a depth of understanding and compatibility that both thrilled and terrified her. Each step brought her closer to another conversation that would undoubtedly leave her both intellectually stimulated and emotionally uncertain.

. . .

M arcus stood in the Ashworth's morning room, his heart thundering against his ribs as he waited for Katherine to appear. The gentle tick of the mantel clock marked each endless second. He paced before the window, unable to keep still after the tumultuous evening with his mother.

"A widow with a grown daughter," the Dowager had said, her voice sharp with concern. "Really, Marcus, what can you be thinking?"

His response had surprised even himself in its vehemence. "I'm thinking that I love her."

The words echoed in his mind now as he traced the familiar path across the Turkish carpet. Two weeks away on business had only confirmed what his heart already knew. Every port he'd visited, every deal he'd struck, had been colored by thoughts of Katherine - her wit, her grace, the way her eyes sparkled when discussing the stars.

He paused at the sound of footsteps in the hall. The door opened, and Katherine entered, resplendent in deep blue that made her eyes shine like emeralds. Marcus's breath caught in his throat.

"My lord," she said, dropping into a perfect curtsy. "What a pleasant surprise."

"Lady Ashworth," he bowed, drinking in the sight of her. The sapphires at her ears caught the morning light, reminding him of the seas he'd crossed to return to her. "I trust you received the astronomical texts?"

"Indeed." A slight flush colored her cheeks. "Your annotations were most illuminating."

"I had rather hoped..." He stepped closer, propriety warring with the urgent need to decrease the distance between them. "That is, I wondered if you might share your thoughts on the calculations regarding the upcoming meteor shower."

Katherine's lips curved into a knowing smile. "And this required such an early morning call?"

"I arrived back in London only last night." The words tumbled out before he could stop them. "I couldn't..." He caught himself, remembering his mother's warnings about proper conduct. "That is, I was eager to discuss the matter with someone of similar intellectual interests."

"Of course." Katherine moved to the writing desk where several papers lay scattered. "I made some observations of my own while you were away."

Marcus followed, catching the subtle scent of lavender that always surrounded her. Two weeks without seeing her face, hearing her voice, sharing in the quiet moments of mutual understanding that had become precious to him. His mother's words faded against the reality of Katherine's presence.

"I missed you," he said softly.

Katherine's hands stilled over the papers. "My lord..."

"Marcus," he corrected. "Please."

She turned, their eyes meeting. The connection between them crackled like lightning before a storm.

"Marcus." His name on her lips sent a shiver down his spine. "We must be careful."

"I have been careful my entire life." He took her hand, propriety be damned. "I've sailed the world's oceans, built a fortune, fulfilled every duty expected of me. But I have never felt anything like this."

"Charlotte..." Katherine began, but Marcus shook his head.

"Is a wonderful young woman who deserves to see her mother happy." He sank to one knee, still holding her hand. "Katherine, these past weeks have been torture. Every moment away from you felt like an eternity."

Her free hand flew to her throat, eyes widening. "Marcus, what are you doing?"

"What I should have done weeks ago." He pressed her fingers to his lips. "I love you. Your intelligence, your grace, your strength. I love the way you light up when discussing the stars, the careful way you manage your household, the devotion you show to your daughter. I love every aspect of who you are."

"But society..." Katherine's voice trembled.

"Can go hang itself," Marcus tightened his grip on her hand. "I've spent twenty years at sea. I know the difference between safe harbors and true north. You, Katherine, are my true north."

K atherine stared at Marcus, her heart pounding so forcefully she feared it might burst from her chest. His words seemed to hang in the air between them, transforming the familiar morning room into something magical and new. She had spent the past fortnight trying to convince herself that her feelings were merely a passing fancy, that a woman of her age and position had no business entertaining such romantic notions. Yet here he knelt before her, offering everything she had never dared to dream possible.

"I..." Her voice caught as tears pricked at her eyes. All her carefully constructed arguments about propriety and duty dissolved in the face of this overwhelming truth - she loved him. Had loved him, perhaps, since that first moment in the British Museum when he had looked at her not as Charlotte's mother or the Viscountess Ashworth, but simply as Katherine.

Marcus rose to his feet, his movements fluid and graceful despite his earlier display of emotion. He kept her hand captured in his, bringing it to his lips once more. The touch sent sparks of sensation racing along her skin.

"Katherine," his voice was rough with feeling as he pressed a kiss to each of her fingers in turn. "My dearest, most beloved Katherine. Will you do me the extraordinary honor of becoming my wife?"

"Yes," the word escaped her lips without hesitation or doubt. All her usual careful consideration fell away, leaving only the pure, simple truth of her heart. "Yes, Marcus. I will marry you."

Joy illuminated his features, transforming his handsome face into something almost boyish in its delight. He gathered both her hands in his, pressing them against his chest where she could feel the rapid beating of his heart matching her own.

"Say it again," he whispered, drawing her closer.

"Yes." Katherine felt laughter bubbling up inside her, pure happiness spilling over. "Yes, I will marry you."

Marcus released her hands only to cup her face between his palms. His thumbs brushed away tears she hadn't realized were falling. "My love," he breathed, and then his mouth found hers.

The kiss was everything a second kiss should be - tender yet passionate, sweet yet promising more. Katherine's hands clutched at his lapels as she rose up on her toes to meet him more fully. His arms wrapped around her waist, drawing her against him until there was no space left between them.

Years of propriety and restraint melted away beneath the heat of his kiss. Katherine felt dizzy with joy and desire, lost in the perfection of this moment. Marcus's lips moved against hers with increasing urgency, and she responded in kind, allowing herself to pour all her long-denied feelings into this single embrace.

When they finally parted, both breathing heavily, Katherine kept her eyes closed for a moment longer, savoring the sensation. Marcus's forehead rested against hers, his breath warm against her lips.

"I have wanted to do that since the first moment I saw you," he confessed, his voice rough with emotion.

Katherine opened her eyes to find him watching her with such tenderness it made her heartache. "And I have wanted you to," she admitted, a blush heating her cheeks at her own boldness.

His answering smile was radiant. One hand came up to trace the curve of her cheek, as though he couldn't quite believe she was real. "My brilliant, beautiful Katherine. How did I live so long without you?"

She turned her face to press a kiss against his palm. "We found each other now. That's what matters."

"Yes." Marcus gathered her close again, and Katherine went willingly into his embrace. She rested her head against his chest, listening to the strong, steady beat of his heart. His chin settled atop her head, and she felt him press a kiss into her hair. "Now and forever, my love."

CHAPTER FOURTEEN
CHARLOTTE

Katherine's heart fluttered as their carriage pulled up to Lady Hutchinson's townhouse. Marcus sat across from them, his presence filling the small space with an energy that made her fingers tingle where they rested against her silk evening gown. The sound of violins drifted through the evening air, accompanied by the cheerful chatter of arriving guests.

"Lady Hutchinson has outdone herself," Marcus observed, his eyes catching Katherine's with a warmth that made her grateful for the dim carriage interior. The pearl ring he'd slipped onto her finger mere hours ago felt both foreign and perfectly right.

Charlotte bounced in her seat. "Look at all the carriages! There must be hundreds of people attending."

As their carriage drew to a stop, Marcus stepped down first, offering his hand first to Charlotte, then to Katherine. His fingers lingered against hers a fraction longer than strictly proper, and she felt the ghost of his touch even after he'd released her.

The grand entrance hall blazed with hundreds of candles, their light reflecting off gilt frames and crystal chandeliers. Ladies in jewel-toned silks swirled past, their gentlemen escorts creating a tableau of black and white evening wear against the colored gowns.

"Miss Ashworth," Lady Constance Whitmore appeared before them, her crimson gown setting off her dark hair to dramatic effect. "How fortunate you are to have secured Lord Rutherford as an escort this evening." Her smile didn't reach her eyes as she turned to Marcus. "My lord, I've saved you a space in my dance card."

Marcus's expression remained pleasant but distant. "I'm afraid my card is quite full this evening, Lady Whitmore. I've promised my dances to the Ashworth ladies."

Lady Constance's smile tightened. "Surely you can spare one dance for an old friend? We had such stimulating conversations at Lady Jersey's ball last week."

"I remember no such conversations of note," Marcus replied, his tone cooling further. "If you'll excuse us, I believe I hear the opening strains of the first set."

Katherine pressed her lips together to hide her smile as Lady Constance drew back, clearly stung by the dismissal. Charlotte didn't bother hiding her gleeful expression as Marcus led them toward the ballroom.

The massive room pulsed with energy and music. Couples lined up for the first country dance, ladies' fans fluttering like butterfly wings in the warm air. Katherine felt Marcus's hand at her lower back, a subtle touch that sent warmth spreading through her body.

"I suppose we should maintain proper distance," he murmured, his voice low enough that only she could hear. "Though I find myself wishing to announce our news to every person in this room."

"Patience," Katherine whispered back, even as her heart leaped at his words. "Let Charlotte have her triumph tonight. There will be time enough for our news later."

As if summoned by her name, Charlotte turned to them. "Mother, Lord Rutherford, look who's just arrived! It's Lord Ridlington."

Katherine watched her daughter's eyes track the young men's progress across the room. The simple joy in Charlotte's expression reminded her of her own happiness, carefully contained beneath her composed exterior.

"Shall we join the set?" Marcus offered his arm to Katherine while nodding to Charlotte. "Miss Ashworth, I believe Lord Ridlington is making his way to secure your hand for the dance."

As they took their places in line, Katherine caught Lady Constance watching them from the edge of the ballroom, her dark eyes narrowed in calculation. The other woman's lips curved in a practiced smile as she caught Katherine's gaze.

"I see Lady Whitmore hasn't given up hope yet," Katherine murmured as they turned through the first figures of the dance.

Marcus's hand brushed hers as they crossed paths. "She never had cause for hope in the first place. My attention has been firmly fixed elsewhere since my return to London."

The music swelled around them, and Katherine allowed herself to enjoy the moment - the brush of Marcus's hand against hers during the turns, Charlotte's laughter floating across the set where she danced with Lord Ridlington, the secret joy of knowing that soon she would have the right to claim Marcus's attention openly and always.

Lady Constance made one final attempt as they paused between sets, gliding up to Marcus with practiced grace. "My lord, surely now you can spare a moment? I've been meaning to discuss the charitable endeavor I mentioned..."

"Lady Whitmore," Marcus's voice carried just enough edge to make several nearby dancers turn their heads. "I believe I made myself clear earlier. My attention and my dances are spoken for this evening—and all evenings to come."

A flush crept up Lady Constance's neck as she registered his meaning. Her eyes darted between Marcus and Katherine, widening slightly before she composed herself with visible effort. "I see. How... delightful for you both." She retreated with as much dignity as she could muster, her crimson skirts swishing against the polished floor.

Charlotte's heart fluttered as Lord Ridlington bowed before her, his hazel eyes warm with genuine pleasure. "Miss Ashworth, might I have the honor of this dance?"

She offered her gloved hand with practiced grace, noting how his fingers trembled slightly as he took it. "Of course, Lord Ridlington. I would be delighted."

As they took their places in the set, Charlotte caught sight of his grandmother beaming at them from her perch among the other matrons. The older woman's approval sent a pleasant warmth through her chest. This was exactly how things should be—a proper young lord, a respectable family connection, everything her mother had worked so hard to achieve.

The music began, a lively country dance that sent them weaving between the other couples. Lord Ridlington moved with surprising grace for someone who claimed to prefer his books to ballrooms.

"You dance beautifully," he said as they joined hands to turn. "Though I confess, I'm grateful it's not a waltz. I fear I would embarrass us both."

Charlotte laughed, the sound bright and genuine. "Surely you jest. I've seen you navigate far more complex figures than a simple waltz."

"Perhaps, but none so nerve-wracking as—" His words cut off as they separated for the next figure, and Charlotte found herself facing down the line of dancers.

That's when she saw him.

Albert Carmichael, the gold in his brown hair catching the candlelight ... was dancing with Lady Sophia. His head was bent close to hers as they turned, his smile intimate and engaging— the very smile that had set Charlotte's pulse racing at their last encounter.

The music suddenly seemed too loud, the room too warm. She watched as Albert whispered something that made Sophia laugh, her friend's face lighting up with pleasure. The same pleasure he had once directed at Charlotte.

"Miss Ashworth?" Lord Ridlington's voice seemed to come from very far away. "Are you quite well?"

Charlotte realized she had missed her cue in the dance. She forced her feet to move, trying to recapture the lightness she'd felt moments before. But her eyes kept straying to Albert and Sophia, drawn like a moth to a flame that would surely burn her.

They looked perfect together, she thought bitterly. Sophia with her quiet grace and Albert with his easy charm. *When had that happened? How had she missed the signs?*

"I fear the heat..." Charlotte managed, her voice barely steady. "Would you be terribly offended if I asked to stop?"

Lord Ridlington's face creased with concern. "Of course not. Allow me to escort you to—"

"No!" The word came out sharper than she intended. Charlotte modulated her tone. "That is, I wouldn't wish to spoil your evening. I simply need a moment of air. Please, continue without me."

She didn't wait for his response, didn't care that her hasty exit would set tongues wagging. All she could see was Albert's hand at Sophia's waist, the way her dearest friend looked up at him with shining eyes.

Charlotte pushed through the crowd, barely registering the worried glances cast her way. Her vision blurred—with tears or anger, she wasn't sure which. She had thought, after their encounter in the rain and their quiet conversations at various parties, that Albert... but clearly she had been wrong.

The sound of Albert's laugh carried across the ballroom, and Charlotte's steps quickened. She needed to escape, to find somewhere private where she could collect herself. Where she could piece back together the dreams that had just shattered like fine crystal on a marble floor.

Behind her, she heard her mother call her name, but Charlotte pressed on. She couldn't face her mother's knowing sympathy, couldn't bear to see understanding in those green eyes. Understanding that would surely turn to disappointment when she realized her daughter had developed feelings for someone so clearly unsuitable.

Charlotte escaped to the terrace and pressed herself against the cool stone pillar, grateful for its solid presence as her world seemed to spin around her. The night air carried the scent of Lady Hutchinson's prized roses, and above, the stars winked down at her with silent sympathy. She drew in a shaky breath, trying to steady her trembling hands.

The image of Albert and Sophia dancing together kept replaying in her mind like a cruel magic lantern show. His hand at her waist, the way he'd bent his head to whisper in her ear, Sophia's delighted laugh—each detail carved itself deeper into Charlotte's heart. She pressed her fingers to her temples, willing the pictures away.

"Stupid, stupid girl," she whispered to herself, the words catching in her throat. "Of course, he would prefer Sophia. Sweet, proper Sophia who never puts a foot wrong or speaks out of turn."

The dance music drifted out through the French doors, the familiar strains of a waltz now seeming to mock her. Charlotte thought of all the times she'd imagined dancing with Albert, how she'd practiced the steps in her bedroom, dreaming of the moment he would hold her close.

What had she done wrong? Charlotte ran through every interaction they'd shared, searching for the misstep that had led him to turn his attention elsewhere. *Had she been too forward at Lady Jersey's ball? Too reserved at the Millbrook's musical evening? Perhaps she should have laughed more at his jokes, or shown more interest in his stories about his grand tour.*

The garden below beckoned, its shadowy paths promising escape from the brightness and music that now felt like daggers to her senses. Charlotte gathered her skirts, ready to flee down the terrace steps into the welcoming darkness.

"Miss Ashworth?"

Albert's voice froze her in place. He stood in the doorway, his figure silhouetted against the warm light from the ballroom. Charlotte's heart performed a painful leap in her chest as he stepped onto the terrace, his familiar scent carried to her on the evening breeze.

"I saw you leave rather suddenly," he said, moving closer. "I wanted to be certain you were well."

Charlotte remained pressed against her pillar, uncertain whether to flee or stay, her pulse thundering in her ears like a drum at execution.

Charlotte's throat constricted as she struggled to find her voice. "I am perfectly well, Mr. Carmichael. The ballroom was rather warm, and I needed a moment of air." She lifted her chin, trying to project a composure she didn't feel.

The night air hummed between them, thick with unspoken words. Charlotte could hear the rustle of his evening clothes as he shifted his weight, could smell the bergamot and sandalwood of his cologne. The scent brought back memories of their dance at Lady Jersey's ball, how his hand had felt at her waist, how his smile had seemed meant only for her.

"Perhaps I could entertain you with a story from my grand tour?" Albert's voice carried a teasing lilt. "I don't believe I've told you about the time I accidentally insulted an Italian countess by complimenting her cat?"

The lightness in his tone sparked something in Charlotte's chest —a hot, burning sensation that rushed up through her throat. "How dare you?" The words burst from her like water through a broken dam. "How dare you stand here and jest with me after— after—" She gestured wildly toward the ballroom, where the music continued to play. "After dancing with my dearest friend like that!"

Albert's eyebrows shot up. "Like what, precisely?"

"You know exactly what I mean! Whispering in her ear, making her laugh..." Charlotte's voice cracked. "Tell me true—are you in love with Sophia?"

A strange expression crossed Albert's face. "Are you in love with Lord Ridlington?"

The question caught Charlotte off guard. She stared at him, mouth slightly open, the anger draining from her as quickly as it had come. The silence stretched between them, broken only by the distant strings of the orchestra and the gentle rustling of leaves in the garden below.

Albert stepped closer, close enough that Charlotte could see the flecks of gold in his brown eyes. "I danced with Lady Sophia because I needed to know something." His voice was low, intimate. "I needed to know if the sight of me paying attention to another woman would affect you as deeply as seeing you dance with Lord Ridlington affects me."

Charlotte's heart stumbled in its rhythm. "You mean..."

"It worked rather spectacularly, I'd say." A smile tugged at the corner of his mouth. "You fled the ballroom as if it were on fire."

"You were trying to make me jealous?" Charlotte wasn't sure whether to be outraged or flattered.

"I was trying to confirm what I already hoped was true," Albert reached for her hand, his touch sending sparks through her gloved fingers. "Charlotte Ashworth, I have been in love with you since the moment you agreed to walk with me in the rain. Your wit, your spirit, your beauty—everything about you has captured my heart completely."

He sank to one knee, still holding her hand. Charlotte's breath caught in her throat as he looked up at her, his eyes shining with emotion in the starlight.

"Will you do me the very great honor of becoming my wife?"

EPILOGUE

CHRISTMAS ~ ONE YEAR LATER

YORKSHIRE

Snow dusted the windowpanes of Rutherford Hall as the family gathered in the drawing room, a fire crackling merrily in the hearth. The past year had brought more joy than Katherine could have imagined, from her intimate wedding to Marcus to Charlotte's grand celebration with Albert just weeks later.

Now, as she sat beside her husband on the settee, watching Charlotte and Albert exchange loving glances across the room, Katherine's heart swelled with contentment. The Dowager held court from her favorite armchair, while Lord Timothy had settled into an unexpected friendship with Marcus's brother Thomas.

"Your turn, my dear," Albert said, presenting Charlotte with an exquisitely wrapped package. She tore into it with unrestrained enthusiasm, revealing a delicate pearl and diamond bracelet that matched her wedding set.

"Oh, Albert!" Charlotte exclaimed, throwing her arms around his neck. "It's perfect!"

Katherine reached for a carefully wrapped package beside her. "And this is for you, my dear Countess."

The Dowager's eyes lit up as she unwrapped the leather-bound journal, its pages filled with pressed flowers and botanical drawings from her prized gardens. "Katherine, you remembered every bloom! Even the troublesome roses that refused to flourish until you suggested moving them to the eastern wall."

"I had help from your gardener," Katherine admitted with a smile. "He kept excellent records of your instructions."

Her hands trembling slightly, Katherine withdrew a small package from her skirts. "And for you, my love."

Marcus took the package, his eyes twinkling. "Let me guess - another set of nautical instruments to replace the ones I supposedly misplaced?"

Katherine gave a nervous laugh, her cheeks flushing. "Not quite."

The room fell silent as Marcus carefully unwrapped the small box. Inside, nestled in silk, lay a silver baby's rattle with the Rutherford crest engraved upon its handle. He stared at it, uncomprehending.

The Dowager leaned forward, squinting at the object. Her eyes widened, and she let out a piercing squeal that made Lord Timothy jump. "Good heavens, I believe I need my salts!"

"Katherine?" Marcus's voice was barely above a whisper as he lifted the rattle from its bed of silk. "Are you certain?"

She covered his hand with hers, her eyes shining. "Dr. Andrews visited this morning. He confirmed what I've suspected these past weeks."

Marcus's face transformed from confusion to wonder. "A baby? We're to have a baby?"

Charlotte clapped her hands in delight. "I'm to be a sister? Oh, Mama!"

The Dowager dabbed at her eyes with her handkerchief. "A grandchild! And here I thought this Christmas couldn't possibly improve upon last year's celebrations."

Marcus pulled Katherine close, pressing his lips to her temple. "You amazing woman. How long have you known?"

"I've had my suspicions since November, but I wanted to be certain before telling you." Katherine leaned into his embrace. "Dr. Andrews says all is well, though he advises I rest more than I have been."

"Then rest you shall," Marcus declared, his voice thick with emotion. "Even if I must tie you to that chaise lounge you're so fond of in the library."

"I rather think that would defeat the purpose of rest," Katherine murmured, making him laugh.

Albert raised his glass. "To the Earl and Countess, and to the newest Rutherford!"

"To the newest Rutherford!" the family echoed, their voices full of joy and love.

Lord Timothy, who had remained quiet during the exchange, finally spoke up. "Well, Marcus, it seems you've managed to give me yet another reason to visit more often than I'd planned."

"As if you needed an excuse," the Dowager sniffed. "Now, Katherine dear, you must tell me everything. Have you had any cravings? When does Andrews expect the blessed event?"

Katherine smoothed her skirts as she settled back onto the settee beside Marcus. "Dr. Andrews believes the baby will arrive in late July or early August. He says everything appears perfectly normal for this stage."

The Dowager's expression shifted from joy to concern as she studied Katherine more intently. "My dear, perhaps we should move this conversation somewhere more private." She rose from her chair with remarkable agility for a woman of her years and gestured toward the adjoining morning room.

Katherine squeezed Marcus's hand before following the Dowager, leaving the others to their cheerful chatter about the baby's arrival. The morning room held the lingering warmth of the afternoon sun, its yellow walls creating a cozy sanctuary from the snow-laden world outside.

"Now then," the Dowager said, settling into a delicate chair and patting the seat beside her. "Let us speak plainly. At your age, childbearing carries certain risks that cannot be ignored."

Katherine smoothed her skirts as she sat down. "I assure you, I am well aware of the concerns. Dr. Andrews was quite thorough in his examination and recommendations."

"Dr. Andrews is an excellent physician, but I remember all too well the difficulties my own sister faced when she bore a child at six-and-thirty." The Dowager's fingers worried at the lace of her cuff. "The strain nearly took them both."

"Dr. Andrews has already prescribed a regiment of bed rest and gentle exercise." Katherine placed her hand over the Dowager's restless fingers. "He believes that with proper care and attention, there is no reason to expect complications."

"And what precisely does he mean by 'proper care'?" The Dowager's sharp eyes missed nothing as she examined Katherine's face for signs of fatigue or distress.

"I am to rest frequently throughout the day, particularly in the afternoons. No vigorous activities or extended social engagements." Katherine couldn't help but smile at the doctor's particular emphasis on that point. "He was most insistent that I avoid the more energetic country dances I'm so fond of."

The Dowager's lips twitched. "I should think so. And what of your charitable work? Surely you cannot continue traipsing about London's less savory neighborhoods in your condition."

"Marcus will help, of course, and Mrs. Winters has agreed to oversee the daily operations of the foundling home." Katherine straightened her shoulders. "I need not abandon my duties entirely, merely adjust how I fulfill them."

"Hmph," the Dowager's expression softened. "You have given this considerable thought, I see. But promise me you will not overtax yourself. Marcus would be quite impossible to live with if anything were to happen to you."

"I promise to be careful." Katherine laid her hand over her still-flat stomach. "Dr. Andrews says the first months are the most crucial. Once spring arrives, he believes I may resume many of my normal activities, though at a more sedate pace."

"And what of the birth itself?" The Dowager leaned forward, her voice dropping. "Has he discussed the possibilities?"

"He has engaged a midwife who specializes in attending older mothers." Katherine met the older woman's gaze steadily.

"Between them, they have delivered dozens of healthy babies to mothers my age and older."

The Dowager sat back, some of the tension leaving her shoulders. "Well, at least he's not taking any chances. I suppose I cannot fault his preparations, though I still wish you were a decade younger."

"As do I, sometimes," Katherine admitted. "But then I think of how much richer my life is now than it was ten years ago. I have Charlotte happily settled, a husband I adore, and now this unexpected blessing."

"Yes, yes, all very romantic." The Dowager waved her hand, but her eyes were suspiciously bright. "But you will humor an old woman who has come to love you as her own daughter. Promise me you will rest when you are tired, eat when you are hungry, and send for Dr. Andrews at the first sign of discomfort."

"I promise." Katherine reached over to embrace the older woman. "And I count myself fortunate to have such a vigilant mother-in-law to keep watch over me."

"As well you should." The Dowager sniffed, patting Katherine's hand. "Now, shall we return to the others before Marcus sends out a search party? He's already hovering like a mother hen, and you're barely three months along."

"What is this mystery, mother?" Marcus asked, his grey eyes twinkling with unrestrained delight as he settled into the chair beside the Dowager. His commanding presence filled the intimate drawing room, yet his expression held all the eagerness of a young boy awaiting a special treat.

The Dowager clapped her hands together. "A summer baby! How delightful. We shall have to arrange for extra awnings in the garden, and perhaps that fountain in the east courtyard needs repair. The sound of running water is so soothing in the heat."

Lord Timothy struck a match, preparing to light his evening cigar. The sharp sulfur scent barely had time to dissipate before Charlotte's face went stark white. She clapped a hand over her mouth, her eyes widening in panic.

"Charlotte?" Albert reached for her arm, but she was already rushing toward the nearest decorative basin, retching violently into the painted porcelain.

Katherine leaped to her feet, hurrying to her daughter's side. She gathered Charlotte's curls away from her face with one hand while rubbing soothing circles on her back with the other. "There, there, my dear. What have you eaten today?"

Charlotte lifted her head, her complexion ashen. "Nothing since yesterday afternoon. I cannot seem to keep anything down these past few days. Even the smell of toast this morning sent me running."

Katherine's hand stilled on Charlotte's back. She turned slowly to face the Dowager, whose expression had transformed from concern to knowing delight. The two women burst into peals of laughter, drawing bewildered looks from the men.

"Good heavens," the Dowager declared, setting aside her sherry glass. "It seems we are to be doubly blessed this summer."

Albert's mouth fell open. "Doubly blessed? What do you mean..."

"She means," Katherine said, helping Charlotte to a nearby chair, "that you and Charlotte should perhaps begin discussing nursery arrangements of your own."

"Nursery arrangements?" Albert repeated faintly. Then understanding dawned across his features. "Charlotte, are you...we're..."

Charlotte's eyes widened as she processed her mother's words. "But surely not... although... oh! The toast, and the carriages making me dizzy, and..." She pressed her hands to her still-flat stomach, wonder replacing her earlier distress.

"Two grandbabies?" The Dowager dabbed at her eyes with her handkerchief. "The Lord truly smiles upon this family. Though I daresay we shall need to ban cigars from the house entirely until both babies arrive."

Lord Timothy hastily extinguished his cigar in a nearby ashtray. "My sincerest apologies, Charlotte. I had no idea."

Marcus wrapped an arm around Katherine's shoulders as she returned to his side. "Well, my love, it seems our child shall have a cousin nearly the same age. What better Christmas gift could we ask for?"

"Two babies," Albert whispered, still looking thunderstruck as he knelt beside Charlotte's chair. "We're going to have a baby."

Charlotte took his hand, pressing it to her middle. "We're going to have a baby," she repeated, her voice trembling with joy.

The Dowager rose from her chair, commanding attention as only she could. "Well then, we must have a toast. Lord Timothy, would you be so kind as to ring for some lemonade? I believe our mothers-to-be would prefer that to champagne at present."

Katherine squeezed Marcus's hand, watching as Charlotte and Albert lost themselves in whispered conversation, their faces glowing with happiness. "To think, a year ago I worried about Charlotte's future, and now here we are."

"Indeed," Marcus murmured, pressing a kiss to her temple. "It seems our season of second chances has brought double the blessings we could have ever imagined."

THE END

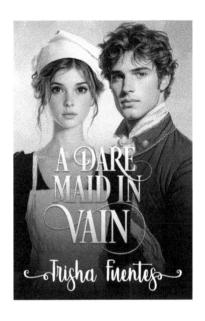

BEST-SELLER!
A MARRIAGE OF MISMATCH

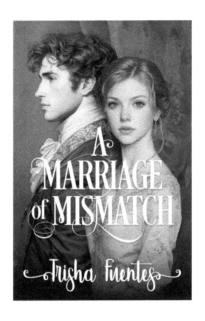

A SCANDALOUS REGENCY ROMANCE

When rebellious Viscount Oliver Thorne is caught in a scandalous situation, his family forces him into a marriage of convenience with the prim and proper Lady Eleanor Cavendish. Oliver is determined to make Eleanor's life miserable, but as they spend more time together, he begins to question his preconceived notions. Will their clashing personalities lead to love or disaster?

Key Features:

- Historical Romance: Immerse yourself in the glamorous world of Regency England.

- Forbidden Love: Explore the tension between a rebellious Viscount and a proper Lady.
- Unexpected Twist: Discover a heartwarming tale of love and redemption.

Get lost in a world of passion, intrigue, and unforgettable characters.

Available in

Ebook & Paperback

SERVICE DAUGHTER SERIES
YOUR NEXT SERIES

HARDSHIP SHOULDN'T HAVE TO BE SUCH AN UPHILL BATTLE

Meet Louisa, Caroline & Hannah

Three daughters born into service. Each with their own story to tell and happily ever after. Simple, ordinary and untitled, unnoticed by the wealthy, struggling with how to survive, how to obtain joy...much less a husband.

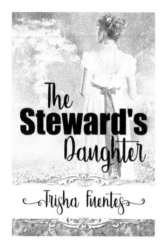

ALL LOUISA WANTED WAS TO BE USEFUL...

The only child of Mr. Ralph Hadley, Land Steward to the Earl of Monbossom, Miss Louisa Hadley lives in a small cottage on the Monbossom estate with her father. When she accidentally breaks her foot after dismounting a horse she is forced to stay in the main house while her father tends to the Earl abroad. With the family now responsible for Louisa's well-being, the classes have reversed as Louisa is constantly scorned by her friends in service. Her circumstances take a more dramatic turn when she stumbles upon the Earl of Monbossom while saving a duckling.

When did he return from France? And who knew his eyes were so blue?

Book 1
Ebook & Paperback

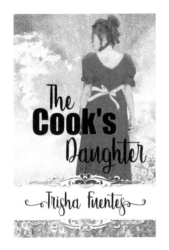

CAN A KITCHEN MAID FIND TRUE HAPPINESS?

Miss Caroline Bates began working in the kitchen with her mother when she was twelve. Caroline grew up with the children of Wellsbury Hall, and watched Lord Gretner's eldest son, Alfred court several noblewomen until one day he finds Caroline practically naked in a nearby moor river.

Is Caroline ruined for all eternity or does she use this mischance to her advantage?

Book 2
Ebook & Paperback

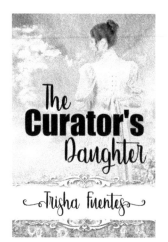

WHICH PATH TO FOLLOW?

The only daughter of a curator of St. Anne's Church, Miss Hannah Pickering grew up knowing she was going to become a nun until she is introduced to one of her father's parishioners. Tempted by the handsome widower who attends her father's church, Hannah is suddenly forced to make a worrisome decision.

Book 3
Ebook & Paperback

ABOUT TRISHA

Hey, it's Trish...

I'm a Romance Author of 40+ books, plus a Publishing House Owner of 50+ Pen Name Authors.

I've been writing romance with a whole lot of heat lately. I love to write fun, fast romances with witty leading ladies getting that gorgeous, sexy, yet lovable guy that doesn't take months to finish. Happily Ever After with a little bit of love angst in between. Whether you yearn for Historical or Modern, I always have a story for you!

Rejoice, Romance Reader...

For upcoming releases, book news, and other goodies,

subscribe to my Newsletter!
https://bit.ly/49BR3UB

instagram.com/authortrish

amazon.com/Trisha-Fuentes/e/B002BME1MI

facebook.com/booksbyTrish

youtube.com/theardentartist

ALSO BY TRISHA FUENTES

❋❋ Series ❋❋

HOLLINGER

Dare To Love - Book 1

A Matchless Match - Book 2

Arrogance & Conceit - Book 3

Impropriety - Book 4

SERVICE•DAUGHTER

The Steward's Daughter - Book 1

The Cook's Daughter - Book 2

The Curator's Daughter - Book 3

THUNDERBOLT

The Surprise Heir - Book 1

A Dance of Deception - Book 2

Win the Heart of a Duchess- Book 3

OBSESSION

Unsuitable Obsession - Part One

Broken Obsession - Part Two

ESCAPE

Swept Away - Book 1

Fire & Rescue - Book 2

The Domain King - Book 3

AGE•GAP•ROMANCE

Whispers of Yesterday - Book 1

His Encore, Her Ecstasy - Book 2

Against the Wind - Book 3

SERIAL • ROMANCE

The Rekindled Flame - Book 1

The Power of Two - Book 2

Facing the Past - Book 3

Taking a Chance - Book 4

Choosing the Future - Book 5

➡**Full Paperback**

https://bit.ly/3XbNK2e